What other readers are saying about
The Miracle of EDSA

The author, Bill Edwards, has placed his fictional characters and wonderful story right in the middle of the action that actually took place during the peaceful struggle to overthrow President Marcos' dictatorship. I recommend this book to freedom lovers everywhere, so they too will fully understand the courage and faith of the people of the Philippines in re-establishing democracy.

—Connie B. Gaspar, Columnist
The Manila Bulletin USA

The Miracle of EDSA is a well written work with an eye for dramatic details, riveting twists of events and character portrayals. Very cleverly done and creative! Suspenseful, and irresistible to put down once you start reading.

I congratulate Bill Edwards for this wonderful and absorbing masterpiece of fiction which will be well received by all readers.

—Tom J. Ilao,
Author of the award-winning book,
America Under Siege: The Drug Invasion

Dedication

This work of fiction is dedicated to the memory of
Benigno "Ninoy" Aquino; to his widow, Corazon
Aquino, ex-president of the Philippines; and to the
courageous people who faced the Filipino Armed
Forces with faith in God as their only weapon.

Acknowledgments

I thank my critique group for their valuable contributions to the preparation of this novel for publication: Virginia Crill, Laura Leonard, Evelyn Sanders, Inga Ferris, Midge Shusta, Dorothy Brendlen and David Sabosky. Thanks to Roberta Tennant, Editor-in-Chief of Falcon Books, for final editing.

Chapter I

Leigh Jackson strolled along the lighted sidewalk toward the nurses' quarters, her mind on a six-year old patient who had just died. She didn't notice the piles of soggy leaves that hadn't been collected last autumn, nor the new foliage already sprouting on poplar trees lining the unkept hospital lawn. Why couldn't they have saved little Ruthie? She heaved a forlorn sigh, sniffed, then blew her nose.

She walked past an automobile parked on the opposite side of the desolate street, unconsciously hearing the starter grinding. Though it was unusual for a car to be here at this time of night, Leigh thought nothing of it. Suddenly, its engine roared into life, tires squealing in protest as it made a quick getaway.

Leigh glanced over her shoulder. The driver was heading directly at her, and my God, he was getting close. The car jumped the curb. Under the glow of the street lamp, Leigh glimpsed the stern-jawed determination on the face of the man behind the wheel. She leaped behind a poplar, into a pile of soggy leaves. The car side-swiped the tree, careened off, then turned back onto the street and sped into the night.

Covered with wet muddy leaves, Leigh jumped up, raised her fist. "Why the hell did you do that?"

Maybe the driver was stoned, and the car got away from him. Like hell. That bastard had her glued in his sights. She headed for a phone at the hospital entrance to report the incident. A police car drove up, and a plainclothes officer got out.

"Are you hurt, Mrs. Jackson?"

"No, but that dude scared hell out of me."

"I'm Detective Sergeant Ashley," the man said, flashing his badge and identification card.

After telling the detective what happened, Leigh waited impatiently for his response.

"Mrs. Jackson, I doubt he was deliberately trying to run you down."

"Damn it, Sergeant, he swerved across the street and aimed right at me." Hands on hips, Leigh Jackson glared into the eyes of the lanky six-foot detective.

"He couldn't have missed you if he really wanted to run you down. You think the driver was Filipino? Did you get a look at the license plates?"

"Maybe, I don't recall the number. But I'll see his ugly face in nightmares the rest of my life. If he had come at me before I got to this row of trees, he would have had me."

"You're absolutely right. He would have run you over before you got this far if he had wanted to, but he didn't. Probably high on booze or pills, or both."

"As I remember, he had trouble getting his car started. And that's why he didn't take a run at me before I got to the trees. How did you get here so soon?"

"I was in the area on another assignment and saw what happened."

"You saw what happened? Why didn't you go after the son-of-a-bitch?"

"Had to make sure you were all right. Maybe you better re-think some of your off-duty activities. Going to rallies opposing the policies of the President of the Philippines isn't setting well with some of his supporters. This may be a warning."

How did Sergeant Ashley know so much about her? Maybe he was following her because her husband had put pressure on the police department. That was it. Alex was looking for ammunition to bring to court in their pending divorce.

"How do you know what I do during my spare time?"

"Everyone in Washington knows about the beautiful wife of a right-wing State Department official speaking out at those Communist meetings."

"They're not Communists. Besides, Alexander Jackson is my ex-husband—well, almost my ex-husband."

"Yes, ma'am. Here's my card. Call me if you remember the license plate number. You'll feel better after you get out of that dirty white uniform and have a hot bath. It was white, wasn't it?"

"Of course it was white. And so were my shoes before I jumped into those wet leaves to avoid being killed."

Detective Sergeant Ashley drove away grinning. Leigh stomped up the walk to the nurses' quarters. Hands trembling, she unlocked the door to her apartment. The phone was ringing. Another call from someone selling something, or was it bad news? She didn't want to talk to anyone. Almost getting killed and losing her favorite patient was too much for one day. Leigh set her purse on the entry table, pulled a tissue from her pocket and looked in the mirror. Her honey-colored complexion had paled under the ordeal. She wiped away the mascara running into her swollen eyes.

"Wish that damn phone would stop ringing."

Leigh removed her soiled white cap and set it beside a vase of yellow roses, sniffing them as she did each day. They reminded her of the flower garden in front of her home in the Philippines. She removed bobby pins, let her long blue-black hair fall onto her shoulders. She brushed away twigs and leaves, gnashing her teeth. Would that ringing ever stop? She got a beer from the refrigerator, pressed the cold can against her forehead, then opened it and took a sip. Leigh finally snatched the jangling instrument off the hook.

"Hello."

"This is the overseas operator. I have a collect call for Leighanne Lincoln Jackson from Rosalita Lincoln Navarro in San Carlos, Philippine Islands. Will you accept the charges?"

Leigh jerked the receiver away from her ear, stared at it. My God, it had been years since she heard from Rosa. Why would she call now? She hated to admit it, but Leigh owed her estranged elderly sister far more than a long-distance telephone call.

"I'll accept the charges."

"Your party's on the line."

"Hello, Rosa. Must be something important after all these years."

"I called because my priest insisted."

Hostility in her sister's voice. Same old Rosa. Still filled with anger. Leigh twisted the ends of her hair around a finger, pulled out a damp leaf and dropped it into the trash.

"How'd you get my number?"

"Never mind, just listen," Rosa said. "I'm sick, and Father Fernando insisted I confess to a lie I told you."

A sob at the other end of the line. Oh Lord, was this a dying confession?

"Do you need money for medical treatment?"

"Medical treatment won't help. Do you remember when we had our babies at that hospital in the hills?"

Leigh flushed, recalling the embarrassment of giving birth to an illegitimate child—a child that had died.

"Yes, I remember. What did you lie about?"

Leigh waited for an answer. The operator came on the line. "We've lost the connection. I'll call you back."

Leigh stayed near the phone, sipping beer. She took a cigarette from a full pack, put it in her mouth and struck a match, hesitated, then blew it out. It had taken her too long to quit smoking when she had returned from Vietnam. She put the cigarette back in the package and paced the floor, drinking beer, thinking about her final argument with Rosa.

All teen-age girls have trouble living under the same roof with domineering parents. Rosa—middle-aged then—had raised Leigh after Mama died. Their problems, however, had been worse than generation-gap disagreements. Both had been pregnant at the same time, and had gone to an isolated hospital for the birth of their babies. Leigh left home months earlier to avoid scandal, working as a kitchen helper to pay room and board. Right on schedule, Rosa's son was born healthy. Leigh, however, was informed her child had been stillborn. She had gone to her sister's room seeking comfort.

"I feel so empty, Rosa," she said. "I know it was embarrassing to you—me being pregnant and not married—but I couldn't help it."

"Come on, Leigh, you've been throwing yourself at boys since you were twelve years old."

"I have not. I was raped."

"Don't lie to me. You've been playing around with some boy after school."

"It wasn't a school boy," Leigh replied. "Your husband raped me."

"Why, you lying slut. Raul couldn't have raped you. I'll take a switch to you for saying such filthy things."

The ringing phone brought Leigh back from her thoughts of twenty-one years ago. She grabbed it.

"Your party's on the line," the operator said.

"Rosa, are you there?"

"Yes, it's me. I don't have much time, but I've got to settle this thing. Father Fernando told me I must confess to lying to you."

"What did you lie about?"

"I bribed the nurse to tell you your baby died. That was a lie, but that's all I'm going to say."

Leigh's child was alive? Was that what Rosa had said? Her baby—the one she had thought dead—was alive?

"Rosa, what did you say?"

"The baby ah-ah-b-b-boy you thought had died at birth is still alive and well."

"My God, how could you have done such a nasty thing? Where is he?"

"I'm not going to tell you any more after your lies about Raul. I did what my priest ordered and that's all I'm going to say about it."

"Is that your dying wish? You want me to spend the rest of my life searching because... Rosa? Rosa?"

The line went dead. Leigh clicked the receiver, called the overseas operator, drumming her fingers, thinking of the baby she had believed dead. It would be almost twenty-one years old now. Where could he be? The doctor who delivered the child might know. What was his name? She must have known at one time. Couldn't think of it now. Leigh shook her head. The hospital was now in guerrilla territory, controlled by hostile anti-Marcos rebels. Impossible to find without her sister's help. Maybe Rosa's son, Virgil, would know? Leigh shook her head. No, she must return to the Philippines and make Rosa tell her.

Chapter II

Daniel Webster Hanks handed his ticket and diplomatic passport to the United Airlines agent. He fingered the faint scar across his ruddy cheek, then clasped his hands together to keep them from shaking. This mission was so exciting his imagination was running wild. It had been a long time since he felt so good about an assignment. His boss had ordered him to stay close to Leigh Jackson. He must, however, calm down. Dan smiled, exposing brilliant white teeth.

"Mr. Hanks, I have to move someone so you can sit beside Ms Jackson," the buxom middle-aged ticket agent whispered.

"Thank you," he replied, brushing reddish sandy hair from his eyes. "She's an old friend. Haven't seen her in years. You're certain it's not too much trouble?"

"Not at all. She will be pleased to have an old friend sitting beside her."

"I'm counting on renewing our relationship."

"That will be nice. You're all set, Mr. Hanks. Have a good trip."

After getting on the plane and buckling her seat belt, Leigh turned out the overhead light, closed her eyes, unaware of the tall fair-skinned man following her down the aisle, then taking the seat beside her.

Sometime after take-off, turbulence woke her. She glanced at her seat companion. He looked familiar, even in the darkened cabin. Trim mustache, receding hair line, scar on his cheek, just like Daddy's and—and the man she had dated in nurses training, Dan

Hanks. The one who dumped her when his wife, who had run off with another man, came home. She had then gone to Vietnam to get him out of her mind and, on the rebound, married Alexander Jackson. Could it really be Dan Hanks? Leigh turned on the light.

"Good to see you again, Leigh," Dan said, running a hand through his disheveled hair.

"This is really a coincidence, Dan."

A puzzled expression crossed her face. Lord, how she had loved this man. His teen-aged son, however, had been so happy his mother returned, Leigh accepted her loss as in the best interests of the boy. Should she ask about them? She squirmed. Not now.

"You're more beautiful than ever, Leigh."

"Thank you," she said, flushing.

Was he trying to sweet-talk her into picking up where they left off? No, Dan always said nice things. Though it made her uncomfortable now, she had missed those compliments. She could have lived without them in her failed marriage, but Alex's constant criticism was too much. There was no way she would get mixed up with Dan Hanks again. Leigh looked out the window into darkness, smiled sadly, then turned to him.

"What have you been up to? Are you still with the San Francisco Police Department?"

"I left them years ago."

"What are you doing?"

"Working for a congressman. You've been raising hell with my boss—and his friends in the administration—at those anti-Marcos rallies. Criticizing martial law in the Philippines hasn't made you popular in Manila either. Why do you do it?"

"Many people feel the same way. Unfortunately, they're not in the U.S. government."

"What I meant was, you're the wife of a conservative official in the State Department. Doesn't he object?"

"Of course he objects. That's why we decided to call it quits. I was tarnishing his image. How does a San Francisco policeman get a job with a congressman in Washington?"

"Two years after you left me, I was looking through the want ads for a moonlighting job so I could send my son to Stanford. I read an article that said my platoon commander during the Korean War was in the hospital at the Presidio."

What had Dan meant, after she left him? Damn it, he dumped her.

"So you went to Letterman Hospital at the Presidio?"

"Uh huh. Colonel Skarlotta was in good spirits despite an injury in Vietnam that cost him a foot. He was pleased to see me, but he asked so many questions I became suspicious."

"Suspicious of what?"

"They were the kind of questions I would ask when investigating a crime. I finally pinned him down, and Fred admitted he was interviewing me for a job. I was hooked after discovering it paid triple my police salary, but I didn't like the location."

"Where was it?"

"Vietnam. I became Fred's field investigator. He was my contact with a congressional committee that was looking into profiteering."

Should she ask about his wife and son? A nagging uncertainty gnawed Leigh. Better wait. She squirmed again, then tried to block her feelings by going over the trouble she had preparing for this trip.

Getting a leave of absence hadn't been a problem. Money was another matter. Rosa was so stubborn she wouldn't voluntarily tell her anything. Leigh would be forced to bribe government officials to dig into records. And as Dan said, she wasn't popular in Manila. She let Alex have their home for $16,000 cash and a promissory note for the balance. That house was the one thing she wanted to hold onto. The agreement, however, settled the last obstacle to their divorce.

After stopovers in San Francisco and Guam, and a delay for typhoon weather, Leigh's plane neared Manila. Returning home filled her with both euphoria and apprehension. Would immigration officers let her enter? Why not? She had a valid passport. Then she noticed Dan looking at her.

"Something wrong?"

"You've slept most of the way. Hope you're rested enough to have dinner with me tonight."

"I must take the first bus to San Carlos, Dan. It's been ten days since my sister called."

"Is she ill?"

Leigh nodded. "By the way, you didn't say why you're headed for Manila."

"To meet my boss. He's on a fact-finding junket."

"You like working for a congressman?"

"Yes, but he's too nosy. Hope he doesn't find out I went to your anti-Marcos rally last month. How did you get started with those people? You always hated Communists."

"I still do, but they're not Communists. Anyway, my nephew wrote about the horrid atrocities near my home town, enclosing pictures that turned my stomach. I wanted to learn more about what was happening in the Philippines. When I understood the people at those meetings were not Communist sympathizers, I made it a point to attend every month."

"I got there early and heard you sing the national anthems. You still have a lovely voice, Leigh."

Leigh smiled. "Thank you. Former Senator Ninoy Aquino was responsible for me becoming a regular. A year ago he suggested I fill in for a guest speaker who canceled."

Leigh clasped her hands together, then unfolded them. The conversation was making her uneasy. "Did you finish your investigation in Vietnam?" she asked.

"Not entirely. We stayed with it after the war ended. Two years ago, however, everything fell apart."

Leigh saw a look of sadness in Dan's eyes. Something was wrong. She waited for him to continue.

"Terry received the clinching proof to convict the profiteers. We were going to turn the evidence over to Fred Skarlotta, catch a military plane to Arizona and lay low until the trial."

"Your son was working with you?"

"He took a leave of absence from the San Francisco District Attorney's Office to get that last bit of evidence against a company in the Bay Area. He and his mother went out to the car while I called Fred, and..."

"And what?"

"I heard an explosion, ran out and saw my car in flames. It blew up when Terry started the engine."

Dan's eyes became misty. Leigh started to say something, but was interrupted by a flight attendant announcing preparations for landing in Manila.

Later, while waiting for her suitcase, Leigh called the bus terminal. The last carrier to San Carlos had left for the day. She dialed several hotels before finding a vacancy. Leigh pulled her bag off the conveyor belt and took it to Immigration, where officials eyed her suspiciously. Getting information about her lost child would be impossible if everyone was as hostile as these dudes. She wouldn't be welcome in any government office.

Leigh and Dan shared a cab into the City, she getting out at the old Admiral Dewey Hotel. When she reached her room, she picked up the phone.

"I want to call San Carlos."

"The lines are down."

"When will they be repaired?"

"Maybe tomorrow."

Nothing was going right. My God, it was hot and humid. Leigh pulled the blouse away from her sticky skin.

"When are you going to get the air conditioning fixed?"

"The engineer is working on the hotel generator."

"Send up a cold San Miguel and a pack of cigarettes."

It wasn't even noon. Well, one beer wouldn't hurt. That was the limit she had placed on herself in her battle against alcoholism. Seeing children killed and maimed in Vietnam had brought a drinking problem, a common ailment among survivors. But why had she ordered cigarettes? She certainly wasn't going to start smoking again.

A knock on the door. She let a bell boy enter with a package of Lucky Strikes and a six-pack of San Miguel. She opened one bottle and drank it, letting the cigarettes lie on the desk, eyeing them longingly, strolling to the window, hoping for a cool breeze. It was calm, not even a hint of fresh air. She opened a second San Miguel, put the cold bottle against her head and closed her eyes. She drank it, then paced the floor. Picking up a magazine to fan herself, she opened a third beer, took a sip and set it down. Her head ached, her stomach was upset. The telephone rang. She grabbed it. No one on the line. Maybe a nap would get rid of the headache.

The phone rang again. The line was still dead. Perhaps the secret police were checking up on her. That detective in Washington could have been wrong when he said they were just warning her. Coming back to the Philippines may have been a mistake. Her ex-husband had told her that Marcos' people would get even for Leigh's public criticism of martial law. Would the police pick her up for questioning? Damn it, she was going to stay here until she found her son.

Leigh's stomach boiled, rebelling against that last beer. Oh Lord, why the hell did she drink it? As the phone rang again, she dashed into the bathroom and vomited. Gasping, she rinsed her mouth with Scope, spit it into the lavatory basin. She felt a little better. If only the pounding in her head would let up. Hey, someone was banging on the door. Secret police? Reluctantly, Leigh opened it. Dan Hanks stood there eyeing her with unmistakable concern. In rust-colored suit, tie and white shirt he was so handsome her heart skipped a beat.

"Thought I'd better come to your room when you didn't answer the phone, Leigh. You were down in the dumps this morning. Had to be sure you didn't do anything foolish."

"Like what? Well, you might as well come in."

He stepped into the room, looked around, then sniffed and shook his head.

"This place smells like a brewery. What have you been doing, taking a self-pity trip?"

"The air-con is off," Leigh replied. "Dan, I have a headache and my stomach can't take aspirin."

"Nerves? You have good reason to be up-tight after the things you said about Marcos."

Leigh felt her face glow with anger. Then she noticed Dan standing with knuckles on his hips. That was what Daddy always did when he scolded her.

"Can you get something for my headache?"

"I'll be back in a few minutes with the only thing I know that'll help. While I'm gone, take a shower, preferably cold, then we'll go to dinner."

Leigh frowned, saluted as she had with her father. Dan scowled, wagged his finger in her face. That was also what Daddy would have done. Leigh smiled despite her annoyance.

"Be right back," Dan said.

Leigh was putting the finishing touches on her make-up when he returned. She had taken the cold shower, but not by choice. The demands of other guests had been too much for the antiquated hot water system in the old hotel. The air conditioning, however, had come on line. Dan appraised her, giving his approval with a whistle. His look made her uncomfortable. She straightened her bra straps, pushing them under her dress. Dan took three small bottles from a bag, poured the contents into a glass, then filled it to the brim with mineral water and handed it to her. Leigh drank the foul-tasting liquid. It settled her stomach, but the headache persisted. She popped a breath mint into her mouth and picked up her purse.

A half hour later, they entered the restaurant atop an exclusive hotel.

"How did you get a reservation here?" Leigh asked.

"Through Congressman Williams." Dan lifted the vase of roses sitting in the center of the table, peered at the flowers, then moved them aside. "Can't see your beautiful face with these between us."

He dropped his napkin on the floor, took a long time to retrieve it.

"Couldn't get hold of this damn thing," he said, sitting up, running a hand through his hair.

As they ate, Leigh wanted to ask Dan why he really came to Manila. Fact-finding had sounded like a lie. She accepted the cigarette and light he offered, then snubbed it out after one puff. Why the hell had she taken that damn thing?

"You said you were still in investigative work similar to Vietnam," Leigh said. "Why is an American sticking his nose into Philippine affairs?"

"At the request of Marcos' opposition."

Leigh sucked in her breath, glanced around, expecting to see police headed toward them. Before martial law, President Marcos welcomed, even relished competition from political opponents. Now he hated—perhaps feared—anyone who disagreed with him.

"Don't say things like that. Remember where you are."

"You're the only one who can hear me, Leigh. I looked the place over for bugs when we sat down."

"So that's what you were doing under the table. Maybe I'll tell the police what you said."

"Like hell you will. I checked you out. I know what you stand for. I'm surprised you dared come here after your public tirades against Marcos in Washington."

"I have good reason to be here, but I've had some doubts since arriving. Hey, what do you mean, you checked me out? So it wasn't coincidence you being in the seat next to me?"

"Easy now, Leigh, don't get riled until you hear what I have to say. You're not safe here, but I know you won't leave until you finish your business with Rosa Navarro."

So Dan knew her sister's name. What else did he know? "I'm getting on that bus in the morning."

"Okay, Leigh, I only want you to take a message to Miguel Morales."

"That Communist!"

"Not so loud. We're probably being watched."

"All right," she whispered, her breath quickening. "Why should I do you a favor?"

"We'll protect your sister and her son by getting them out of the country."

"What makes you think they're in danger?"

"I saw a list of people targeted for the death squad. Virgil Navarro's name is on it."

Oh my God, her nephew was more involved in guerrilla activities than she had realized.

"All right, I'll deliver the message to Morales if you'll protect my sister and nephew, and one other person."

"Who?"

"Tell you later, Dan. Got to get up early. Please take me home."

In the cab on the way to her hotel, Dan opened her purse and slipped an envelope inside. Leigh frowned, started to say something, then realized Dan didn't trust the driver. She looked at him questioningly.

"Not here," he whispered.

When the cab stopped, he escorted her to the entrance, planted a kiss on her cheek and left. A kiss on the cheek? A tinge of disappointment swept over her. Why? The past was dead, her affair with Dan long forgotten. Besides, she came here to find her son, nothing else. Leigh sighed, picked up a newspaper when she got her key, then took the elevator to the third floor.

In her room, she undressed and turned on the bed-side lamp, wrinkling her nose at the smell of stale beer. She emptied the open San Miguel bottles, washed them out and tossed them in a trash basket. Then she took the envelope out of her purse and set it on the bedside stand. She propped herself up in bed, glancing at the envelope as she read the newspaper. Dan's picture was on the front page with a group of pro-Marcos American congressmen. Which side was he working for? Leigh threw the paper across the room and turned out the light.

"If the police caught me with a message to a Communist leader, they'd throw me in prison for the rest of my life," she mumbled.

And that would likely be a very short time in the hands of Marcos' interrogators. Leigh turned on the light, picked up the envelope and ripped it open. A letter, hand-written in—oh my God—Russian? She must get rid of it. Still, if she didn't take the message to Morales, Rosa and Virgil would be killed. She struck a match, burned the envelope, hesitating over the letter. Her own son might be involved in guerrilla activities along with her nephew, and his life could also be in danger. Leigh took out a comb and brush and went to work on her long hair. Later, she turned out the light, the message—torn in half—hidden in two tight braids.

Chapter III

Troubled by what she might have to do to get Rosa to tell her where to find her son, Leigh couldn't sleep. She came up with one answer, discarded it for another, then another, finally realizing nothing would convince her sister to cooperate. She eventually dozed, tension, however, bringing restless sleep.

When the wake-up call came, Leigh answered the phone. Still tired, she yawned, put her head back against the pillow and closed her eyes. Suddenly, she sat up, looked at her watch. 6:30 A. M. My God, she'd miss the bus. No, Filipino buses were usually thirty minutes late. Still, she jumped into her clothes, checked out of the hotel and caught a cab to the terminal.

"The bus left on time?" Leigh gasped, shaking her head. "I can't believe that."

"It happens," the ticket agent replied. "The bus was overloaded anyway, so we set up another one. It'll stop at the corner on EDSA."

"EDSA?"

"Epifanio de los Santos Avenue," he whispered.

"I know what EDSA means. Why not here?"

"Shh, not so loud. It's a special bus. Eight o'clock. Don't be late."

Leigh walked away, frowning, shaking her head. Why was the ticket agent so secretive about his special bus? After eating breakfast, she carried her bag to the ten-lane wide thoroughfare. At eight thirty, a maroon bus—the words Philippine Rabbit painted on the side barely visible under the dirt—pulled up to the curb. The other passengers turned their heads away when she walked down the aisle. Maybe they had heard of her anti-Marcos activities and didn't

23

want to get involved? Overhead racks and empty seats were filled with packages, shopping bags and suitcases. She sat in a rear seat.

Exhaust fumes made sleep impossible. Bumper to bumper traffic crawled along the thoroughfare. The jeepney beside them—a highly polished black with red and yellow scrolls on the hood and sides—was overloaded with children squeezed onto bench seats facing one another. They had casts on their arms and legs. Leigh smiled, waving as the jeepney turned onto a side street. The kids waved back.

When the bus got out of the city, the driver took a secondary road. Leigh slept until it stopped for lunch. She ate, got back on the bus, then dozed until they entered San Carlos. Once a little country town, it was now bustling with activity.

"Good Lord, look at this place," she mumbled.

Soldiers marched around the old municipal building, their headquarters. Others entered bars, cafes and banks, or churches, movie theaters and market places.

After the passengers got off with only their suitcases, the bus pulled away. Why had they left packages and shopping bags aboard? Puzzled, Leigh strolled away, looking for a ride to Rosa's house. Jeepneys were overflowing. She started to walk the two kilometers when one of her sister's neighbors pulled up in a horse-drawn caratila.

"Thank you for stopping, Mr. Concepcion. I'm glad you remember me," Leigh said.

"Who could forget such a pretty girl? You broke a lot of hearts when you left for California."

Leigh threw her bag aboard, climbed up and sat beside the old man. "I hope not."

"Glad you came home, Leigh," he said. "Rosa's too sick to take care of your Daddy's place."

"Is your family well?"

"Well as can be expected." He raised his sombrero, wiped the sweat from his brow on a bandana.

At the edge of town the odor of farm animals wafted into her nostrils. Though she had hated the stench as a child, Leigh was overjoyed now. She had come back to her childhood home. As they neared Daddy's old frame house, her smile faded. A paint job couldn't correct all the deterioration. Storm shutters were missing, siding rotted, even a section of the roof had blown away. Flowers and shrubs had been destroyed. Cane fields lay fallow. Leigh hurried up the walkway, crossed the veranda and opened the door. She smiled sadly, sniffed the air. No cooking odor. She glanced at her watch. Six o'clock. As long as Leigh could remember, Rosa had prepared dinner at this time.

Relieved she didn't have to face her sister so soon, Leigh, however, felt the disappointment of another delay. She looked in the kitchen to be certain Rosa wasn't there, then checked upstairs. No one. Maybe she was visiting a sick friend. Leigh hurried downstairs, then went through the kitchen to a roofless veranda. A tall attractive young woman hung wet clothes on a line.

"Who're you?"

"My name's Marci," the young woman replied, straightening up to her full height, nearly as tall as Leigh, sweeping long black hair behind her ears with one hand. "Are you Mrs. Navarro's sister?"

"Yes, I'm Leigh Jackson. My nephew wrote about you, Marci. Where's Rosa?"

"Mrs. Navarro went to see Virgil this morning and hasn't returned."

"Where is Virgil?"

"In the hills."

"Why?"

Marci didn't answer, clasping, then unclasping her hands, glancing around furtively.

"Marci, I'm not a spy. Didn't Virgil tell you about me?"

"Yes, but I'm nervous." The young woman managed a weak smile. "The police accused him of being a Communist."

"Oh Lord, I was afraid of something like that. Do you know how to find my sister?"

"Mrs. Navarro went to the forest north of town. A path leads to Virgil's camp."

From the way she talked, Marci was too well educated to be a maid. Why was she working in such a menial job?

"I'll change clothes, then you can show me the way."

"It'll be dark soon and the trail is too dangerous at night. Soldiers and guerrillas shoot at anything that moves. We must wait until dawn, then sneak past the guards."

Leigh returned to the living room, picked up her bag and carried it to the bedroom she had used until she was sixteen. She glanced at photographs on the dresser, picked up the last one taken of the family on her father's seventy-second birthday. As her fingers moved across the picture, caressing his weather-beaten face, she sniffed back tears. Daddy was so patient, the nicest person she had ever met.

Leigh blew her nose, got a back pack from the closet, then checked medical supplies, jungle fatigues and combat boots. She had left them here on returning from Vietnam, her first visit since running away from home. It was her only attempt to reconcile with her sister after Raul, who raped her, had died. Leigh shook the fatigues, tried them on. A little snug in the hips, but better than a dress for hiking. She filled the pack, hesitated over a bottle of perfume, then put it in the plastic bag with lipstick and make-up.

"Damn, almost forgot my machete."

Daddy had given her the two-foot long knife when she worked with him in the sugar cane fields. Being beaten—and almost raped again—as a senior in high school, Leigh carried it everywhere. She had also dedicated herself to physical fitness and karate, determined never to be unprepared again. Leigh got the machete from her bag and set it beside the back pack, then returned to the kitchen.

"I've been thinking," Marci said, folding her hands as if praying. "Mrs. Navarro might have taken the wrong fork in the trail and ended up in Sumo's camp."

"Who?"

"Huge kid, about Virgil's and my age. Sumo's a little taller than you and I, but he's as big as a Japanese Sumo wrestler. He tried to steal Mrs. Navarro's chickens last month, but she blasted away at him with a shotgun."

"He's probably carrying a grudge. Let's hope she didn't run into him." Leigh yawned. "Wake me early enough so we can get by the soldiers before dawn."

The next morning, Marci roused Leigh. After dressing, they made their way under fading moonlight. As they passed through sugar cane fields, Leigh wanted to cut off a piece to chew on, but feared the noise would rouse soldiers in a nearby camp. They hiked across dikes separating rice fields, swatting mosquitoes swarming off the water, reaching the edge of the forest shortly before sun up.

"Virgil's camp is an hour and a half up this trail," Marci said. "Take the path to the right at the fork. Sumo's camp is to the left."

"You've got to come with me, Marci."

"The Chief of Police is sending an officer to the house to check on a report that Mrs. Navarro is missing. Someone has to be there."

Too impatient to wait until dawn, Leigh began hiking as soon as Marci left. As the trail entered the hills, it started a shallow climb. Leigh passed by lava and limestone outcroppings, meadows of tall coarse grass and thickets of bamboo shoots. She smiled going through groves of palm trees, recalling how, as a child, she had shucked coconuts, splitting the shells and drinking the milk. The trail steepened, tree cover thickened. She sniffed the air. Ah, the lovely smell of mahogany. Why had she ever left this beautiful place?

Leigh continued another half hour, stopped to catch her breath, then sat down on a fallen tree, wiped the sweat from her brow and took a long drink of water. Rosa couldn't have come this far. Maybe Virgil met her, and she was too sick to go home, so he took her to his camp. What if she had run into that chicken thief? As Leigh stood up, nearby bushes rustled.

Chapter IV

As Leigh grabbed the handle of her machete, a teenage boy stepped out from behind foliage, rifle aimed at her chest. She moved her hand away from the sheathed weapon. Snarling, the youngster, dressed in jungle fatigues, gestured. A group of guerrillas, about the same age, surrounded her.

Forcing a smile, Leigh raised her hands. These kids would probably release her when they learned her nephew was also a guerrilla. Should she tell them? Not now, they were too hostile. The leader grabbed her machete, formed Leigh and the kids into single file, then set out at a blistering pace. Were they running from soldiers or trying to break her spirit? The muscles in her legs cried out. Her whole body ached for a breather, but she was determined to keep up. A sharp pain stabbed her side. Leigh fell back. A youngster prodded her with his rifle barrel. She clenched her teeth, kept moving. No way would she let them know how much she hurt. They finally slowed to a brisk walk.

"So you are human," she gasped.

The kid behind Leigh snickered. Why had they been pressuring her? Maybe they thought she hadn't shown them proper respect and were trying to teach her a lesson. The new pace gave her a chance to look around, filing landmarks in her memory. When the trail split, they took the left branch, stepping over or jumping rivulets of water trickling across the path. The streams flowed toward the sound of rapids. A fast-flowing river? Multi-colored parrots flew from one tree to another. Discreetly, she kicked the trunks and broke twigs on bushes to mark the trail.

They hiked across meadows of tall coarse grass and wild flowers, then through groves of bamboo, nipa and coconut palms. Leigh stored them in her memory. They finally skirted a lava rock outcropping resembling the back of a camel, and entered a camp. She reached for her canteen. A guerrilla grabbed it. He and a companion hustled her to a nipa-hut on stilts. She climbed the ladder, crawled onto a mat covering a bamboo floor. They tied her hands and feet.

"Hey, give me some water."

They left, ignoring her plea. Leigh looked around. Four disheveled blankets lay on top of mats as beds. The stench of stale sweat lingered in the air. Photos were tacked on bamboo walls beside tattered shirts and pants. Small bundles of personal items sat beside each bed. She was now a prisoner of a bunch of dirty angry kids. Well, she had to come into these mountains to find Rosa, and to deliver Dan's message to Morales.

The hut swayed. Some one was climbing the ladder. A huge young man, as big as a Japanese wrestler, crawled in, then stood up, wielding a machete. Four or five years older than the kids, he still looked baby-faced, except for the wrinkles of anger running across his brow. The stench of his sweat was so strong, Leigh turned her head.

"What's on your mind?" she asked.

Eyes blazing, he spit tobacco juice toward a can in the corner and missed. Then he brought his long knife down quickly alongside Leigh's neck as if to cut off her shoulder. She flinched. He grinned, raised his machete to chop at her legs. My God, was he going to cut them off? Leigh closed her eyes, gritting her teeth, sucking in air. Her eyelids popped open. Dare she look?

"You son-of-a-bitch," she cried out involuntarily.

Still, she felt no pain. Glancing down, Leigh noticed he had severed the ropes tying her legs without drawing a drop of blood. Though relieved, she was furious at the cruel hoax. Rage clouded her mind. She must stay cool, but if it was the last thing she did, she would make this overgrown ape pay for his sadistic joke.

"The boss wants to talk to you before I work you over," he said, grabbing his crotch.

Flushing with anger, she struggled onto her feet, then stumbled and fell.

"Having trouble staying on your feet?"

Leigh got up, then moved toward the doorway without comment. The big fat guerrilla cut the ropes binding her hands, jabbed at her back with his long knife, laughing maniacally.

"I'll have you on your back before you know it."

Leigh understood what he meant and knew she had to prepare herself mentally to go up against him. He was too big to handle in a fair fight, even with her skill in karate. She must find a way to attack first, then use every dirty trick she could remember.

She climbed down the ladder, strode up to a scowling young man puffing on a cigar. He was several inches taller than she, over six feet. He sported a shaggy mustache, the color of his stogie, and long black hair, tied in a pony tail. Somehow, he looked familiar. Yes, she had seen his picture in newspapers. So this was Miguel Morales. He was much younger than she had expected, about Virgil's age.

"I came here to give you a message," she said. "Tell one of your juvenile delinquents to get me some water."

"No one comes into these mountains without my knowing. Who the hell are you?"

"Right now, I'm a courier. Please give me some water."

"Sumo, get it," Morales ordered, chomping on the end of his cigar.

"I'm rationing water," the big guy replied. "You've had your chance to talk. I want her back."

So this was Sumo, the one who tried to steal Rosa's chickens. He was a rival to Morales—likely hated it—but didn't have the strength to challenge him.

"Maybe you'll get her back and maybe not," Morales replied. "Look to your right, in that nipa palm tree. You can't see my sniper, but he's there. And there are others all around you. This is my territory. Do you want to start something here?"

Sumo backed away, set his machete against a palm tree at the edge of the clearing, then plopped down on a stump in front of it. Morales handed Leigh his canteen. She gulped a few swallows, then sipped.

"My name is Leigh Jackson. If you'll get my back pack and machete from these kids, then help me find my sister, I'll give you a message from Dan Hanks."

"Hanks? How do you know Dan Hanks?"

"We were—we are old friends. When he learned I was coming to San Carlos, he asked me to bring a letter to you."

"I'll take it."

She hesitated. Could she trust him? Realizing she had no choice, Leigh unfastened her braids, eased the folded papers out and handed them to him.

As Morales deciphered the message, Leigh's thoughts returned to settling her score with Sumo. If she could get his machete, she might chop off one of his toes before he knew what was happening. Leigh sidled toward the long knife. A warning flashed into her mind. Sumo might be inviting her to do something foolish. Be careful. She spotted a pile of coconuts in the clearing.

"Mind if I have a look at your bolo knife?" Leigh asked.

She picked up Sumo's machete, hefted it. About the same weight as hers. Rifle bolts clicked as guerrillas charged rounds into firing chambers. A sweat formed on her forehead. She knew she was pushing her luck, but Leigh strolled to the clearing.

"Easy, Kids," she said, with a calmness that didn't reflect the butterflies swarming in her stomach. "I'm not going to cut off Sumo's balls. Perhaps another time, but not today. A little coconut milk will do us all a lot of good."

It had been years since Leigh shucked coconuts, but she was still proficient with the machete. She sat on the ground, unzipped her boots, then removed them, along with her socks. She rolled her pants legs up to the knees and spread her legs, flexing them so she could grasp a coconut between the soles of her feet. Leigh took a deep breath, swung the long knife overhead and brought it down, chopping into the husk, slicing off a chunk. She swung the machete again and again, stripping away the husk. Leigh tossed the stripped coconut to a grinning youngster. That was the first one. Would both feet still be attached to her legs when she had finished? Leigh wiped sweat from her forehead. Minutes later, she had unhusked all the coconuts in a wild display of skill that made the guerrillas cringe respectfully.

"Guess I'd better clean up this mess," she said, feigning the end of the show. Leigh put on socks and boots, then rolled down her pants legs. She stood up, swung the machete back and forth, spun around and heaved it at the big fat guerrilla. The long knife whistled through the air, thudding into the stump between Sumo's legs, humming, quivering, inches below his crotch. His face paled.

"Thanks, Fatso," Leigh said, striding to Morales as the kids covered their mouths to suppress laughter.

Anger blazed in Morales' brown eyes. "What's in your back pack?"

"Medical supplies. I'm a nurse and got in the habit of carrying them because of my experience in Vietnam."

"Who's your sister?"

"Rosalita Navarro. She came into the mountains searching for her son, Virgil."

A guerrilla ran up to Morales, whispered in his ear. The tall mustached man jogged out of camp, leaving Leigh in the clearing, surrounded by Sumo's hostile youngsters.

Chapter V

Leigh cursed Morales under her breath. She had risked her life to deliver Dan's message, and the guerrilla leader was walking away.

Now Sumo would have a free hand with her. He could rape her—or even kill her—for embarrassing him in front of his men. What could she do? Kick the big ape in the groin and run? Leigh hesitated, glancing at Sumo out of the corner of her eye. The arrogant bastard was smirking. She flushed. Easy now, she must not let rage get the upper hand. She turned back to Morales as he was about to enter the forest.

"Miguel, you owe me," Leigh shouted.

The tall guerrilla leader stopped at the edge of the clearing, a puzzled expression on his face. My God, he had forgotten her! He wiped the sweat from his brow, then beckoned. Leigh ran to him.

"You said you were a nurse. My corpsmen can use medical training." His eyes narrowed. "I don't like pushy women."

"I suppose you like pushy men?"

"No one would dare do to me what you did to Sumo."

"You want yes-men?"

"You're stretching your luck, Lady. I owe Dan Hanks, but shut up or I'll leave you on the trail." He turned. "Get her back-pack, Arturo, we can use the medical supplies."

Arturo ran back to the clearing, grabbed Leigh's pack, then brought up the rear as the group set out at a dog trot. An agonizing hour later, they paused for a breather.

As Leigh gasped for breath, a short slender woman in freshly washed jungle fatigues came out of the woods. Unlike the others, she didn't smell like an old goat. Thank God for that. The woman beckoned. Leigh followed her to a clearing filled with nipa-huts on stilts. They climbed a ladder, crawled in and sat on a floor mat. The scent of fresh flowers wafted gently over the hut. Photos were taped to walls. Ropes had been strung to hang extra clothes. Personal possessions lay next to lighted candles and small statues of the Virgin Mother.

Leigh studied the young woman. Still in her twenties, she had scrubbed her face as clean as her fatigues. Might even be pretty if she used a little make-up.

"My name is Paulita. Miguel said to tell you about your sister. I'm sorry, but she was killed by soldiers."

"I don't believe that."

If it was true, how would Leigh find her son? Virgil was her only link. Oh Lord, he would be heart-broken by the death of his mother, unable to handle her questions. Guilt washed over Leigh as she realized she should be thinking of her nephew's feelings instead of herself.

"My priest was visiting a farmer at the edge of the forest last night and heard about it," Paulita continued. "He took her body to San Carlos."

"I'm too shocked to talk now."

Paulita opened her mouth to say something, closed it, then left. Though she denied Rosa's death, Leigh realized the woman was telling the truth, except maybe about who killed Rosa. Would soldiers dare come into guerrilla territory? Maybe Morales was trying to shirk responsibility. Leigh agonized late into the night, plotting how she would seek revenge without doing anything to jeopardize the chances of finding her son. She finally closed her eyes, grinding her teeth in frustration.

Later, she woke up when the hut swayed, threw off the blanket someone had put over her. Sitting on another bed, Paulita lit a candle, crossed herself.

"What's going on?" Leigh asked.

"That's probably Virgil," Paulita said. "Word spread quickly about his mother, and your nephew headed for San Carlos to take on the whole Philippine Army by himself. Miguel sent someone to bring him back before he was killed."

Paulita rolled her hair into a bun and pinned it in back, then slipped out of the hut when a young man crawled in.

This was Leigh's first meeting with her nephew though they had exchanged letters since he was ten years old, shortly after his father had died. Virgil took after her side of the family, getting his height and strength from Grandpa Lincoln, and a smooth honey-colored complexion from Grandma Lincoln. He wore his long hair in a pony tail, emulating Morales.

"Auntie Leigh," he cried.

She held him as he sobbed softly. He was taking it hard, maybe blaming himself for her death. Would this tragedy plunge him into a depression as the death of his father had? His letters to Leigh had shown he was sensitive, prone to feel the loss of a loved one too long. She had helped him through that difficult period. He was only a kid then, and the boys' school he was attending had been a lonely place.

They held each other for a long time. Finally, he pulled away, wiped his tears on a red bandana.

"Mama would be alive if it wasn't for me. She had only a few months left, but they took that from her."

"It's not your fault, Virgil."

"She didn't understand the danger in these mountains. Wish I had known she was coming."

"We can't let Morales get away with it."

"He didn't kill Mama," Virgil said.

"That's what Paulita told me, but I don't buy it. An aide to an American congressman told me you were targeted by the death squad, but soldiers had no reason to kill her."

"They don't need a reason, Auntie Leigh. It was unusual, but the Philippine Army occasionally comes into these mountains to kill or frighten people who support Miguel."

"I don't trust that Communist."

"Miguel grew up in Mindinao, but he's not a Communist. Don't know where he was born, but his guerrillas are from this area. I've known most of them since we were kids."

"I wondered about his accent. I've been away a long time, but I speak Tagalog more nearly like the others. Even after getting your letters, I still think of anyone opposed to Marcos as a Communist."

"Your American upbringing. President Marcos has so much influence in the United States, they believe his propaganda."

"Wish you had told me sooner what was happening in the Philippines, Virgil."

"I thought about it for several years before I finally got enough guts to join the guerrillas. That's when I wrote you about the atrocities. Anyway, we have to talk about Mama's funeral. As an American citizen, you'll be all right, but I have to go in disguise. When it's over, I'll find the killers."

"Your Mama and I had our differences, but she was family. How can I help?"

"I don't want you hurt, Auntie Leigh."

"I can take care of myself, but I've got to watch out for a big fat guerrilla named Sumo."

"My God, you didn't cross that maniac, did you?"

"Who is he?"

"The illegitimate son of a Philippine Army officer. He was raised by a family named Zurate," Virgil replied.

"Zurate? Where have I heard that name?"

"They live in a village near San Carlos. Sumo has his own army of guerrillas."

"Yeah, a band of dirty juveniles, only a little younger than himself."

"He's the same age as me, Auntie Leigh. And those kids are just a small part of his army."

"Sumo scares me," Leigh said. "I wouldn't turn my back on him, but I think I can handle the slob."

"Watch out for Sumo. In grade school, the big kids picked on him. He held a grudge until he got to high school and had outgrown everyone. Then he broke their arms."

Chapter VI

At dawn, Leigh and Virgil left the nipa-hut. A guerrilla returned her machete and back pack. It was noticeably lighter than when she had entered camp. She opened it. The medical supplies were missing. She glared at Morales.

"We haven't seen antibiotics in months," he said. "I couldn't let you keep them."

Grinding her teeth, Leigh put on her pack. Well, there was nothing she could do. Besides, she owed him.

"Virgil, wait for my okay before going after your mother's killers," Morales continued.

Glancing at her nephew, Leigh was ready to object when she noticed him shaking his head. Virgil put on a pack and started out of camp, she with him. They turned off the main trail, jogging along a steep path, a more difficult route to the valley. Virgil said it would by-pass Sumo's camp. The pace brought cramps to her legs. When they finally stopped, Leigh massaged her calves.

"Virgil, you must speak up when Morales talks to you like you were a peon. Don't let him tell you what you can and cannot do."

"I'm not Miguel's yes-man, but he'll kill me if I interfere with his plans. He'd like to attack the Philippine Army in town, but they're too strong, so he's set up an operation to draw them into the country-side."

"We can't hold off forever."

"I understand that, but you can't get involved, Auntie Leigh. You must leave the Philippines. Otherwise, Marcos' people will hassle you. I need your help, but you'd be useless with them dogging your footsteps."

"I can't leave, Virgil, I have important business."

"You must go. Take a plane for the States and get off at Guam. Come back without going through immigration."

"How will I do that?"

"On our medical supplier's boat. I'll give you his name and address on Guam."

Her nephew was right. She would accomplish nothing with Marcos' secret police hounding her. Should she ask Virgil about her son, nothing insensitive, just enough to pick up a few crumbs of information?

"Did your mother ever talk about other relatives?"

"Papa has a half-brother with a bunch of illegitimate kids. I've never met them, except Sumo."

"I remember her saying something about your father's half-brother." Leigh brushed the hair from her eyes. "By the way, did you have anything to do with that special bus from Manila?"

"Since the Army took over San Carlos, we get supplies any way we can. Friends buy things in Manila, then leave them on the bus."

"How did you know I had arrived in the Philippines?"

"Miguel has a contact in Immigration." Virgil paused. "We're out of Sumo's territory now. Better change clothes."

Virgil opened his back-pack, took out two black priests' robes. Leigh pulled one on over her fatigues.

"Why priests' robes?"

"We might be mistaken for soldiers without them. We can keep our boots."

"I don't look like a man of God."

"I have hats, fake beards and mustaches."

After they had disguised themselves, Leigh still felt she couldn't handle the role. Picking up back packs they set out along a winding down-hill trail. The light-weight robes became unbearable with no breeze and high humidity. An hour later, they reached the valley. As Leigh wiped the sweat from her face, Virgil pointed ahead.

"There's an army camp. Now we walk in and ask for some water."

"Why?"

"It'll look suspicious if we don't. The Church condemns atrocities, but doesn't shun soldiers. Lower your voice if you have to say anything."

Leigh nodded, despite her fear of being unmasked. Virgil greeted a baby-faced soldier guarding the perimeter, asking for directions to the commanding officer's tent.

Oh, Virgil, don't beg for trouble, Leigh thought. Get the water from this kid.

"That way, Father," the guard said, pointing to the largest tent. "Lieutenant Lopez has just returned."

"Thank you," Virgil replied, touching the young man gently on the shoulder.

The soldier looked as if he was going to speak. When Leigh paused, Virgil tugged on her robe. They went to the commander's tent, peered in. A Philippine Army officer sat at a desk, head in his hands. Face ashen, he looked up.

"Come in, Father," he said. "I'm Lieutenant Gregorio Lopez. How may I help you?"

"I'm Father Manuel. This is Father Antonio," Virgil said, striding forward and shaking the officer's hand. "Just a little water, if you please, Lieutenant, then we must be on our way to San Carlos."

Leigh remained at the entrance to the tent, clasping her hands to keep them from trembling. She nodded at the introduction. Virgil's self-assurance made her only slightly less nervous.

"Of course, Father, help yourself. Will you hear my confession before you leave? It's been a month since I've been to church."

"After I quench my thirst. You first, Father Antonio," Virgil said. "Then if you'll wait outside, I'll hear the Lieutenant's confession."

Leigh went to the water bag, dipped out a cup of cool liquid, drained it and another, then nodded her thanks and raced for the exit. Outside she sighed in relief. The soldier who had given them directions ran up. Had she done something to arouse his suspicions?

"Father, please hear my confession," he said.

What had she gotten into? It had been years since she had even gone to confession. The regimentation Rosa forced on her as a child caused Leigh to abandon the Church when she grew up. Now she had no choice.

Leigh lowered her voice. "Of course. Where shall we go for privacy?"

"Into the woods, Father."

Leigh looked into the boy's eyes, spotting his anguish. The kid wasn't more than seventeen years old. And something was tearing him apart. If she could provide some comfort, God would forgive her for acting as one of his servants.

The young man led the way into the woods, stopping beside a bush. Leigh went to the other side, kneeled, then removed a stole from her pocket and draped it around her neck. How should she begin? The soldier didn't wait, spewing out his trouble.

"I have sinned, Father, and I ask for absolution."

"What have you done?"

"We picked up an old woman taking supplies to the Communists. I had to follow orders and k-k-kill her. I didn't want to, but Lieutenant Lopez put a gun at the back of my head."

Was this the soldier who had killed Rosa? "How do you know she was taking supplies to the Communists?"

"That's what the lieutenant said when he pulled off her crucifix."

"Why did he want her crucifix?"

"It was gold, covered with diamonds and rubies."

Now Leigh was certain the old woman was Rosa. In an attempt at reconciliation nine years ago she had given an expensive crucifix as he described to her sister. There couldn't be another like it in San Carlos. If he killed Rosa because he was afraid of being shot, did that mean it wasn't his fault? Then she realized the young soldier had stopped talking. Could she give him an answer without choking on her words?

"That was a dastardly thing to do, killing that poor old woman," Leigh replied.

"Yes, Father. I am sorry for my sin."

"God will forgive you if you are truly sorry for the grief you've caused. You must give penance every day the rest of your life. Now go and sin no more, lest the wrath of God come upon you."

She wanted to rip the kid's heart out. Leigh returned to camp. Virgil was waiting, a haggard look on his face. They headed for town.

"Lopez confessed he ordered his men to kill Mama," Virgil said. "Can you imagine, he wanted absolution?"

"The baby-faced kid confessed he pulled the trigger because the lieutenant held a gun to his head."

"Probably true. Lopez accused the brigade commander of giving the order with the threat of a firing squad."

"Then who the hell is responsible?"

"Marcos, and everyone up and down the line. I felt like sticking a knife between Lopez's ribs."

"Damn these people. Why are they picking on us?"

"We're not the only ones, Auntie Leigh. Remember the Garcias?"

"They own the farm next to ours. Big family, ten kids, as I recall. What about them?"

"Soldiers killed them, even the old folks living there with the son and daughter-in-law who ran the farm."

"Why?"

"For gold the Japanese stole from the countries they conquered during World War II. Marcos' people think some of it is buried on the Garcia farm."

"Your grandfather told stories about it. Leon Garcia and I went looking for gold in the hills between our farms. Did the soldiers kill all of them?"

"The youngest, Max, escaped. He's one of Paulita's guerrillas now. We're almost home, Auntie Leigh. Let's cut through the cane fields. Marci can fix something to eat, then I'll go to the church and stay the night."

A short time later, they exited a field of head-high weeds behind their home. Leigh grabbed Virgil's arm, pulled him back into the thicket.

Chapter VII

"Why did you drag me back into the cane field?" Virgil asked.

"There's a military staff car parked in front of our house. Wonder why it's here?"

"Maybe they're going to take over our farm. I heard Marcos' people are looking everywhere for Japanese gold."

Leigh removed the false mustache and beard, took off her robe, then put everything in Virgil's back-pack. They waited, sitting on the ground, leaning back against dead stalks of sugar cane. Virgil fidgeted with his collar. She smiled, caressed his shoulder. He finally shook his head in disgust.

"It's getting late. I'm going to church."

"I know how you feel, but I have to stay here. Wish I could barge into the house, but not in fatigues."

After he left, Leigh wished she had questioned him more about her son. Maybe Virgil didn't know she had had a child out of wedlock. Could his mother have kept it from him?

Perhaps it was best she didn't ask. Sharing her problems now would only place another burden on him. Maybe there were legal papers in the house that would provide the information she needed. Of course, in Daddy's safe.

As the sun dropped below the horizon, an Army officer came out of the house. A sergeant, idling on the front porch, hurried ahead and opened the rear door of the sedan. Then a huge man ran out and jumped in with the officer. As they drove away, Leigh entered, sneaking up the stairs to her room. She undressed and put on a robe, then picked up her dirty fatigues and carried them to the rear veranda. The maid was working.

"You frightened me," Marci said. "The soldiers didn't see you?"

"I hid in the cane field until they left. Who are they and what did they want?"

"I don't know the general or his driver, but the big fat guy is Sumo. He's supposed to be a guerrilla. I don't know why he was with them. The general said he owns this farm now that Mrs. Navarro is dead. Sorry about your sister."

"How can he claim ownership? Half this property belongs to me. And Virgil should inherit his mother's half as soon as we find her will."

"You saw Virgil? How is he?"

"He came here with me, but was too impatient to wait for the soldiers to leave, so he went to church."

"I fixed fried chicken to take there as Mrs. Navarro does each week. The general said Virgil lost his claim to the farm because he's a Communist."

"Does he know I'm home?"

"He asked where you were. I told him you went to see Father Fernando. The general also said, as a foreigner you couldn't own property in the Philippines."

"Well, he's got another think coming if he thinks he's going to cheat us out of our farm."

"I'll take fried chicken to the church," Marci said.

"Tell Virgil to stay out of sight. Oh, is Daddy's safe still in the master bedroom?"

"In Mrs. Navarro's closet."

After bathing, Leigh slipped into a house coat, then went to the master bedroom and turned on the light. A steel safe took up most of the space at one end of the closet. She dropped to her knees, crawled under the clothes. It was locked. What was that combination? Daddy had used his birth date, or something like that.

Leigh tried every mixture of numbers without success. Better try something else. How about 1946 for her, 1924 for Rosa and 1889 for

Daddy. On her sixth try Leigh hit the right combination, swung the door open. She took out a photo album, ledgers and packages of papers held together with rubber bands. Probably legal documents on the house. She would look them over later. Now she wanted almost anything personal. Oh God, she didn't even know her son's name.

Leigh put the first packet back, picked up the second. Her father's death certificate and U.S. Army discharge papers. Leigh returned them, then thumbed through another file. Raul Navarro's death certificate, Philippine Scouts discharge and medical papers. She set them aside. The next pack contained birth certificates. A signature was scrawled illegibly at the bottom of Virgil's. She sighed, put them with the others on the floor. She would check it later in better light.

The only things left were the photo album and the ledgers. As she debated her next move, Leigh leafed through the album, lingering over pictures. One was of Rosa's husband and another man in a Philippine Army uniform. They looked almost like twins. Was this Raul's half-brother?

Leigh shivered, trying to push aside the memory of the night Raul had come to her room. She removed the picture from the album and turned it over. "Raul and Fidel—October 31, 1961 at the Songbird."

"That was the night he raped me!" Leigh exclaimed aloud.

She had returned to an empty house from choir rehearsal that night long ago. Rosa left a note saying Raul's half-brother had arrived and they were taking him to The Songbird Tavern. Leigh went to bed, waking up when they came home. She went back to sleep as soon as the house was quiet again. Someone crawled in beside her. She turned toward the newcomer, thinking it Rosa who usually slept with her when Raul got drunk. The smell of liquor made Leigh realize it wasn't her sister. Rosa didn't drink.

"Raul, get out of my..."

A hand closed off her mouth. She tried to push him away. He grabbed Leigh's arm, rolled on top of her, spreading her legs with his knees. She tried to throw him off. Then she felt an excruciating pain as he entered her body. She was squirming, struggling, trying to scream. A fist slammed into her jaw. She raked her fingernails down his cheek as darkness closed in around her.

When she awoke, the sun was rising. Her first thought was she had had a horrible nightmare. A chill ran down her spine when she noticed blood on the sheets, and felt an ache between her legs. Raul had raped her.

Even now, Leigh fumed with anger. Then she heard a noise downstairs. What was that? Someone walking through the living room? She put the photo album back in the safe and locked it, then realized she had left some things out. Leigh shoved the picture of Raul and Fidel in one of the ledgers and put them with papers under a pile of sweaters on the shelf. She grabbed a cane from the corner of the closet as a weapon and crept down the stairs.

"Who's there?"

"It's me—Marci. Father Fernando is holding Mass for your sister tonight. We don't have much time."

Early the next morning, Leigh and Marci, in black mourning dresses; Virgil, in priest's robe; and neighbors wearing work clothes, listened to Father Fernando read the scriptures at the grave site. As he closed the bible, and grave diggers lowered Rosa's casket, Leigh glanced around. A Philippine Army general stood on a hill over-looking the cemetery, the same man who had been at her house yes-terday. Why was he here? Her question was answered even as she asked. A squad of soldiers appeared from behind a building. She turned to whisper a warning to Virgil. He was already dodging headstones, racing up the slope toward the safety of the forest. Mili-tary policemen, on off-the-road motorcycles, joined the chase. They disappeared over the hill. Leigh dashed after them.

"Lord, help Virgil," she panted.

The motorcycle riders sped by Virgil, then stopped, turned around. Raising rifles, they opened fire. Caught in a cross fire, Virgil sidled toward the forest, throwing off his robe, firing an Uzi automatic rifle hanging from a strap attached to his shoulder. He went down. Leigh ran toward him. He got up, shooting, hobbling toward the woods. A band of guerrillas appeared at the tree line and opened fire at the soldiers.

"Thank God," Leigh gasped, dropping to the ground, taking cover alongside soldiers.

Mortar shells exploded among the guerrillas. Screams of pain from wounded and dying echoed across the battle field. Virgil and his friends lay dead or injured, but the soldiers continued shooting. Leigh jumped to her feet, wrenched the rifle from a baby-faced soldier, recognizing him as the one who had killed Rosa. Heart flaming with uncontrolled anger, she aimed at the youngster and squeezed the trigger.

Something slammed down on her head, engulfing her mind in a brilliant display of fireworks.

Chapter VIII

As she returned to consciousness, Leigh raised her handcuffed hands to her aching head. What happened? Where was she? In the back seat of a car speeding along a highway. Her stomach was acting up, and she felt woozy. How stupid could she have been, trying to shoot that soldier with his friends surrounding her. She hadn't realized then what she was doing—she was furious at the soldiers for shooting her nephew— now she was too sick to care. Leigh stuck her head out an open window, vomiting into the wind.

She slumped back in the seat and gasped. Three men in the car. An Army general next to her, the one who had been at her home, and had come to the funeral. She had seen him somewhere before. His neatly pressed uniform was covered with awards and decorations. Spit-polished shoes, short-cropped black hair sprinkled with streaks of gray set him apart from the other officers. His flitting eyes, however, reminded her of the man who had raped her. She shuddered.

A sergeant was behind the wheel. The lieutenant sitting beside him also looked familiar. Of course. The bastard who ordered Rosa's death. How could she have forgotten?

"Where are you taking me?" Leigh asked.

"Why did you try to shoot one of Lieutenant Lopez's soldiers?" the General asked, ignoring her question.

"He was going to kill my nephew. What have you done with Virgil Navarro?"

"You admit knowing he was disguised as a priest? That makes you a Communist sympathizer, subject to arrest and imprisonment, not to mention your attempt to shoot a soldier doing his duty."

"I met Virgil at the funeral for the first time. And I had no idea he would be disguised as a priest."

Lopez interrupted. "Why did your nephew try to join the guerrillas who killed his mother?"

Leigh flushed with anger. She was about to accuse the lieutenant of killing Rosa, when a warning from her military training flashed into her mind. Junior officers didn't interrupt generals. He was trying to trick her into admitting she had talked to Virgil before the funeral. Had she taken the bait, it would have been an admission of guilt. American citizenship wouldn't help her if the Philippine government had evidence she supported Communist guerrillas.

"Is my nephew all right?" Leigh winced, rubbing her temple to soothe an aching head.

"He's being held under guard in a hospital. He may not survive, but I'll see that you have a chance to visit him, if you cooperate."

"I've told you everything I can, General. I know my nephew only through his letters. He's not a Communist. He hates them as much as I do. Why have you arrested me? I'm an American citizen."

"I know you are Leighanne Lincoln Jackson, born in San Carlos. And I know you moved to the United States as a young woman, but we found nothing identifying you as an American citizen. I'm General Navarro, Commander of Fort Bonifacio, where you'll stay during interrogation. We'll become well acquainted before you leave the Philippines—if you leave."

Sweat beaded on Leigh's brow. She brushed at it with her sleeve, recalling the old photo of him and her sister's husband at the Songbird. This was Raul's half brother. He was responsible for her sister's death, and he had ordered his own nephew shot. If Virgil died, Leigh would be next. Then there would be no one to dispute his claim to the family farm. Why did he want that old run-down place? Oh Lord, he had said Fort Bonifacio, the prison where President

Marcos confined political enemies. Only those he dared not kill, because of international pressure, left there alive.

"You can't do that. I'm a citizen of the United States. I want to see the American Ambassador."

"If you're an American, where's your passport?"

"In my...where's my purse?"

"Lieutenant Lopez, did you find Mrs. Jackson's purse?"

"My men are still searching the cemetery, Sir."

"We'll soon be at my headquarters. Lieutenant Lopez will take care of you while I attend to another matter. Perhaps his men will have found your identification papers by the time you've been interrogated. If we can verify your claim, perhaps I will release you."

A short time later, the lieutenant led Leigh into a small office, unfastened her wrists, then stood with his back to the door, smirking, pulling up sagging trousers. A stout matron tore the black dress off Leigh. Lopez laughed.

"Hey, what are you doing?"

A matron slapped her. Leigh drew back her arm to hit the woman with a karate chop, then stopped, swallowing, deciding to suffer the embarrassment in silence.

A matron tossed her a baggy prison dress. "Put it on."

Wrinkling her nose at the foul odor of stale sweat, Leigh slipped into the stinking garment. Didn't they wash their clothes? Matrons behind her, Leigh followed the lieutenant down a flight of stairs into a small damp windowless room.

She took a deep breath to steady her nerves. The stench of death hit her like a boxer's knockout punch. She gagged, stomach churning in rebellion. What was this place? The matrons tied her wrists to metal rings attached to the ceiling, pulled the ropes until she stood on tip-toes.

"You can't do this to me," Leigh cried.

She looked around, horrified—yet fascinated—by the instruments attached to a drab gray wall. Black rubber hoses a yard long. Cat-o-nine tails, stained with dried blood. Four-foot long bamboo sticks, human flesh clinging to split shafts, blood dripping down the wall. A pair of pliers, long bloody fingernails on the floor beneath them.

Leigh felt a cold shiver shake her body, goose bumps covering it from head to toe. My God, the room was a torture chamber. This didn't happen in the civilized world. She was an American. They wouldn't dare, would they? The more she denied it, the more Leigh realized she was their next victim.

"Tell me about your nephew's association with Miguel Morales," Lopez said, picking up a rubber hose, slapping it against his open palm, black eyes blazing.

"I don't know anything. I didn't even meet Virgil until this visit. Last time I was here, he was away at..."

She never finished the sentence. The hose slammed against her back, bringing an agonizing pain from neck to waist, air gushing from her lungs. She tried to yell, but could give it no voice. Flailing her legs, Leigh struggled to catch her breath, frantically fighting the ropes holding her off the floor.

She gasped, "Can't do this...I'm an..."

Lopez slammed the rubber hose against her back again. The pain returned, followed by another frightening struggle to breathe. Once more, a voiceless scream stuck in her throat. She lost consciousness. A matron doused her with a bucket of water. Leigh shrieked as air flowed back into her lungs. Was there anything she could do to stop this torture? Her mind raced to come up with an idea. Any story, even if it was false, might stay Lopez's hand. Then she saw his shadow on the wall, raising the club to strike again. She clenched her teeth, anticipating the blow that would surely crack her backbone.

Chapter IX

Before Lopez could slam the rubber hose against Leigh's back again, the door burst open.

"Stop!" Dan Hanks rushed at the lieutenant, wrenched the weapon from his hand and smacked him on the knee. Screaming, Lopez fell to the floor.

"The Second Secretary to the American Embassy is filling out papers for Mrs. Jackson's release," Hanks growled.

Rubber hose still in his hand, Dan cut the ropes holding Leigh to the rings. Blinded by tears, she grabbed the club, wanting to bash in Lopez's face. But her pain was still unbearable. Leigh dropped the weapon. Grimacing, she leaned on Dan as he helped her up the stairs.

Moments later, Leigh sat in a chauffeur-driven limousine between Hanks and an immaculately dressed man with a full head of gray hair. Frederik Skarlotta was as tall as Dan, a little older. She had noticed a limp when he lumbered to the car. Except for nodding when introduced, Skarlotta said nothing. Silence prevailed until they passed through Fort Bonifacio's main gate.

"I know you're going to be in a bind with the Ambassador to explain why you used his name to get Leigh released, but damn it, Fred, she isn't a Communist."

"I'll tell him General Navarro was mistaken when he picked up one of our intelligence agents who pretends opposition to Marcos as a cover. I don't know what to say about her nephew. Shrug it off as something that happens in families, I guess."

"What about Virgil? Is he alive?" Leigh asked.

"I haven't learned anything about your nephew, Mrs. Jackson. You must leave the Philippines right away. After a doctor exams you, Dan will explain why. I'll find out what happened to Virgil Navarro and let you know."

Later, Leigh stepped out of a hot shower, drying her body on a soft towel. Despite the beating, the doctor had said she suffered no permanent injury. Breath quickening at the thought of Dan Hanks, she smiled, then frowned. He had dumped her once. Getting involved with him again would be stupid. Besides, she felt like hell. Leigh slipped on a robe, shuffled into the sitting room.

"Feeling any better, Leigh?"

"A little bit, but I'm too keyed up to sleep. Can we talk? I wasn't planning on staying in the Philippines long, but I don't want to leave until I finish what I came here to do. What did Skarlotta mean when he said I had to get out of the country right now?"

"The Ambassador will buy his story for a while—you being an intelligence agent for a pro-Marcos group—but without a passport he'll fold when General Navarro puts on pressure."

"I have good reason to be here. Besides, the Embassy can call the State Department to prove I'm an American."

"Marcos' people will hound you even with a passport. What kind of business are you involved in that's so damn important? You wanting to stay here and General Navarro torturing an American citizen doesn't make sense."

"Marcos can pressure the State Department to delay giving me another passport. And he can issue a decree authorizing the General to confiscate our farm. But that won't keep me from taking care of my personal affairs."

"Why does he want that damn little farm?"

"For gold the Japanese stole from countries they occupied during World War II. It's buried all over the Philippines. Our farm is a likely place."

"I've heard that old rumor a hundred times. Anyway, it shouldn't take long to get a new passport. Your husband can cut through the red tape."

"He wouldn't even try. And I won't ask."

"You haven't said why it's so important for you to stay."

Leigh sighed. Should she tell Dan everything, or just enough so he won't oppose her?

"I must find my son."

"What?"

"I had a child when I was sixteen. Until recently, I thought he had died at birth."

Dan raised his eyebrows.

Leigh continued. "Rosa told me my baby was stillborn. Just recently, she confessed that was a lie. With Rosa dead, I'm hoping my nephew can come up with some information."

"Your sister wouldn't tell you?" Dan asked, brushing his sandy hair back with his hand.

"We've had almost no contact for twenty-one years. When I accused her husband of raping me, Rosa became furious. I moved to the States to get away from her. Now I don't even recall the doctor's name, nor how to get to the hospital. It's somewhere in the hills near San Carlos."

"I'm sorry, Leigh, you must leave the Philippines. You could hire someone to look for your son, but you won't."

"That's right. I don't trust anyone."

"You have to get out of the country now, Leigh. I know you'll come back, but—for Christ's sake—by-pass immigration. I couldn't stand anything happening to you."

His eyes became misty. Leigh pulled him to her breast. Moments later he raised his head, looked into her eyes. His lips met hers. Her aching body tingled, becoming warm. She was too vulnerable to resist. Dan started to pick her up.

She cried out, "Oh, that hurts."

He stammered an apology, but Leigh led him to the bedroom, then moved to the side of the bed. Dan rushed to her, pulled down the bedspread and sheets, then tore off his shirt. Staring at the scars crisscrossing his muscular chest and abdomen, Leigh slid between the sheets. He needed her, but she knew he wouldn't force the issue. And she did not feel up to making love.

Dan caressed her cheek, kissed the corner of her mouth, then eased himself in beside her. Gently, he took Leigh in his arms, holding her tortured body. She fell asleep, but was awakened several times by claps of thunder. Dan was still beside her, watching over her. She snuggled closer. The phone rang. He rolled onto his side, picked up the instrument and listened. Slamming the receiver down, he jumped out of bed.

"General Navarro's on the way. That son-of-a-bitch got to the Ambassador before we expected."

Leigh jumped up, groaning at the sudden movement. As she slipped into her clothes, someone banged on the door to the sitting room. They hurried to another exit that led to a connecting hallway. Would soldiers be there too?

Chapter X

Dan eased the door open, stepped out, grabbed Leigh's hand. She held her rib cage, stifling a cry of pain. Lord, how she hurt. They hurried along the corridor. Footsteps sounded in the adjoining hallway. Soldiers would come around the corner any moment. Dan pulled her into a stairwell exit, then peeked through the window in the door.

"They're coming," he whispered.

Leigh held her breath, heart pounding, shuddering at the thought of returning to that torture chamber. Clomping footsteps continued past the door.

"Let's get out of here," Dan said.

They scurried down a flight of stairs, listened, then descended three more floors. Suddenly, a door overhead banged against a wall. Dan pulled her away from the railing.

"They could have gone down here," a voice said in Tagalog. "You guys take the elevator."

"What did he say?" Dan asked.

"He's coming down the stairwell, the others are headed for the elevator."

"There's a service elevator at the rear of this corridor. Hope they don't think of it."

They ran to the end of the hallway and pressed the elevator button. Gasping for breath, Leigh held her side. Though it seemed a lifetime, the elevator came up quickly. They descended to the ground floor, ran to a car in the parking lot. Leigh eased her tormented body into the passenger seat. Dan drove away, waiting until he turned onto a side street before switching on headlights. They headed out of town, thunder rumbling as lightning streaked across the dark morning sky. Heavy rain cut visibility to zero. Dan inched along the highway.

Leigh struggled to get comfortable, then closed her eyes. "Where we headed?"

"Clark Air Force Base, American airfield north of here."

Two hours later, Dan drove through the main entrance to a military installation. Bright lights woke Leigh. A sign—Clark Air Force Base—identified it as American.

"Why don't I hole-up here until I feel better?" she asked. "I think that rubber hose smashed my backbone."

"This is an American base, but it's commanded by a Filipino Air Force colonel who takes his orders from Marcos. Fred Skarlotta got you on a medical evacuation plane."

"I can't leave now, Dan."

"For Christ's sake, Leigh, you must get the hell out of this country! I've arranged for you to stay with an old friend on Guam." Dan turned onto the tarmac and headed toward a transport plane.

"Who?"

"Cathy Valentine. Don't talk to anyone until she meets you. I'll let you know about Virgil as soon as I can."

My God, it had been eleven years since she had seen Cathy Valentine, her nursing school roommate, at the University of California Hospital in San Francisco.

Dan led her up the steps of the med-evac plane. A nurse helped Leigh onto a stretcher-bed. After he left, she wished she had stayed awake and questioned Dan during the drive to the air base. Maybe Cathy could fill her in. She closed her eyes, but sleep wouldn't come. Leaving the Philippines with so many problems on her mind was a bummer. Somehow, she must find the doctor who delivered her baby. And poor Virgil. How could she rescue him?

Some time later, the plane's wheels dropped and locked in the down position. The pilot landed, taxied to the parking ramp. A customs inspector boarded as orderlies carried Leigh to an ambulance. It drove away from the flight line. After passing through the main gate of Anderson Air Force Base, Leigh got on her feet, went to the rear door, looked out the window. The driver stopped. Suddenly, the door opened. A tall attractive blond, in an expensive tailored suit, stood with hands on her hips. Leigh stepped down. Groaning, she hugged her former roommate.

"Sorry they beat up on you, Leigh," Cathy said. "I feel responsible. Let me help you."

"It's good to see you again, Cathy. Why do you feel responsible?"

The tall blond ignored the question, put her arm around Leigh's waist, assisting her to a Toyota idling by the side of the road.

"You're still beautiful, Leigh, though you must be pushing forty now," Cathy said.

"Thirty seven next July, and you damn well know it. Your thirty-fifth birthday is only two days after mine, and you still look great."

"Figured I'd run into you after graduation, but it's been eleven years," Cathy said. "Why did you stop writing?"

"I didn't, you did."

"Maybe you're right. I went to Vietnam after graduation, then got lost in a whisky bottle. I gave up drinking when Paul Cummings came into my life. We settled down until he got hurt in an automobile accident. So I went back to work to pay the bills."

Leigh frowned. Cathy was forced to go to work because her husband had been injured? Had her family cut her off? She was still wearing expensive clothes. According to rumors that had floated around campus, she was from a wealthy Mafia family. Cathy, however, always changed the subject when Leigh tried to get her to talk about them.

"Paul's all right now, even went back to work," Cathy continued. "Anyway, I like my job, so I stayed on. But I'm scared to death half the time. I'll tell you about it on the way to town."

"I understand your problem with the booze, Cathy. Had the same trouble when I returned from Vietnam."

"I didn't know you'd been there. Seems to me, you were going to school after serving as an enlisted peon in the U.S. Army, and you were fed up with military life. Didn't think you'd ever go back in, even as a nurse."

"I was in Vietnam for three years with a medical team from the Philippines."

"You spent three years in that place? My God, you must have been a raving maniac when you came home."

Seeing Leigh's misting eyes, Cathy patted her shoulder with an understanding that comes from someone who had been through the same ordeal.

"Tell me about your job, Cathy. Besides Vietnam, what have you been doing?"

"I work with Dan Hanks. Do you still have a thing for him? Poor little Terry. Remember him?"

"I was heart-broken when Dan told me his boy was killed," Leigh replied. "What about the job?"

"We work under contract providing nursing services for air medical evacuation teams in the Pacific area."

"Thought the military took care of its own," Leigh said, glancing at hotels dotting the sky line as they neared the city of Agana.

"We supplement them. Un—ah—Fred Skarlotta recruited me as a nurse for a cover so I could deliver medical supplies to Filipino guerrillas. Dan is my contact."

"Why would an American diplomat recruit you for a job like that?"

"He's a member of an organization determined to overthrow Marcos. It's illegal as hell, but several congressmen are in up to their eyeballs."

"Do you have trouble delivering supplies?"

"Sure as hell do. By the way, I was responsible for you being picked to take the message to Miguel Morales. Didn't know how to get in touch, but Dan Hanks came to my rescue. Sorry it got you in trouble."

"So I have you to thank for my broken back? Besides, you know I hate Communists. We talked about it often enough in training."

"You hate Marcos' people even more, but that's beside the point," Cathy replied. "My middle-man has been siphoning off medical supplies and selling them on the black market."

"You had something else in mind for me other than delivering that message? Come to think of it, you were for left-wing causes in training."

"The insurgents need our help now, and we'll need theirs if we have any hope of getting rid of Marcos."

"How do you plan on getting medical supplies to the Philippine guerrillas?"

"I know how you must feel now, but your nephew's in a bind. And I don't think you're going to stand by and do nothing. I want you to take over delivery to Morales' guerrillas so I can get rid of the dude robbing us blind."

"I'm going back to the Philippines as soon as I feel up to it, but only to find my son."

"You're naive if you think an American passport is going to do any good, Leigh. And you'll have a hell of a time getting another. Besides, Fred will be stonewalled."

Cathy was right. Dan's diplomatic friend would learn nothing. She would be on her own. On the other hand, if she delivered the medical supplies, Morales would be obligated to rescue her nephew. It might delay the search for her son, but she couldn't live with herself if she didn't think about Virgil. Hmmm, Cathy avoided mentioning her family again. Well, that wasn't important now.

"All right, I'll take your supplies to Morales. I don't feel well at the moment, but I'll bounce back. Fill me in."

Ignoring Leigh, Cathy speeded up, passing every vehicle on the highway as they approached the outskirts of Agana.

Leigh frowned. This wasn't like Cathy, driving so recklessly, knuckles white from gripping the steering wheel. She was uptight about something.

"Whoa. What's going on?" Leigh asked.

"We're being followed."

Chapter XI

Leigh looked back, spotted a black sedan weaving from one lane to another. "The Cadillac?"

"Yeah, and I can't out-run them. Get my binoculars out of the glove compartment and check the license number. We can find out later who owns it."

"Got the number," Leigh said, after training the glasses on the pursuers. "Oh my God, the bastard behind the wheel is the dude who tried to run me down in Washington."

"There's a police station up ahead. I'll stop and get in touch with an old friend."

Moments later, Cathy drove into a reserved parking space. "Come on, Leigh."

Leigh hurried into the station behind Cathy as fast as her aching body permitted. "Now what?"

"Go out the side door and catch a cab to the Guamanian Hotel. I'll call tonight and we can go over plans for delivering medical supplies to Morales."

Ten days later, Leigh neared the Philippines on a fishing trawler filled with medical supplies. A typhoon approached as they sailed into the Lingayen Gulf on the northwest coast of Luzon. Because of poor visibility, the captain had Leigh go forward to guide them ashore. She was forced to tie herself to the deck to avoid being washed overboard. The bow dipped into heavy swells, rose high above them, then repeated the violent maneuver again and again. Winds lashed rain against her face like a wet mop. She stared into darkness, shifting her gaze from one side to the other. It wouldn't be long before the full force of the storm would tear the boat apart. Where was that light on shore? For that matter, where was the shore?

"We should have left Guam without the damn first mate," she growled.

Searching bars for the drunken first mate had almost ended in disaster. Leigh ran into pro-Marcos people tailing him. She fled to the medical supply boat, and the captain sailed into bad weather ahead of a typhoon.

Now, as they neared their destination, poor visibility might cause them to end up on the rocks. Was the captain headed in the right direction? Leigh chewed her lip, then spotted a glowing light. Thank God. But they were off-course. The boat would run aground if she didn't warn the man at the wheel. Leigh pulled out a flashlight, shone it aft, moving the beam horizontally. The bow turned. When they were headed toward the beacon, she moved the beam up and down. The boat stopped turning, heading straight for the signal light.

Minutes later—though it seemed forever—they sailed into an area protected by swaying palm trees. Though rain continued, the wind no longer whipped into her face. A shadowy figure kneeled behind a light on another launch. The launch's navigation lights flashed on. It sailed into the mouth of a narrow swollen river. Leigh's medical supply boat followed. The water was relatively calm though river banks overflowed. Leigh untied herself, got on her feet. Wind howling, trees swayed as they sailed into a lagoon to a dock. Leigh jumped off. Staggering on unsteady legs, she headed toward the dim figure kneeling behind the light, finally recognizing Morales' lieutenant. What was her name? Oh yes, Paulita.

"Glad you finally got here," Paulita said. "Let's unload before the typhoon hits."

"Do you have a place we can hole-up?"

"My guys will take the supplies to our cave," Paulita replied.

Leigh followed her to an entrance hidden among shrubbery. A tunnel led to a cavern. The floor was covered with dry bamboo mats, separated into storage, sleeping and eating areas. Not plush, but it would protect them from the storm.

"That's your bunk," Paulita said, pointing to a cot with a blanket and clothing. "You can get out of those wet clothes while I fix chow."

Too exhausted to care, Leigh staggered to the cot, slipped out of her outer garments and collapsed. She slept, oblivious to the storm and the boisterous guerrillas carrying supplies into the cavern.

Several hours later, Leigh awoke, discovering someone had covered her with a blanket. The cavern was lighted by a lamp on a table near the tunnel exit. One man was awake, his ear glued to a radio. She slept again. Moments later—it seemed—Paulita roused her.

"Get dressed and grab something to eat, Leigh. The storm isn't over, but we've got to get out of here."

Leigh put on jungle fatigues too big in the waist and shoulders. Better than wet clothes. Wolfing down cold fish and rice, she slipped on a back-pack, pulled a poncho over her head, then plopped a hat on top and tied the strings.

Picking up a rifle, Paulita went out into the storm. Leigh followed her to a refurbished U.S. Navy motor launch, stowing her pack in the hold with the others. A guerrilla dried spark plugs and wiring, started the engine. After coughing a few times, it ran smoothly. Paulita cast off, heading upstream against wind and rain. Men pushed floating trees aside with long poles. Tree branches, however, tangled in the propeller. The engine stopped. Guerrillas dived overboard, cleared the debris. They sailed upstream again.

"Leigh, keep an eye out for things that'll get tangled in the prop," Paulita yelled.

Minutes later, Leigh spotted refugees clinging to trees floating down-stream.

"Hey, there are people hanging onto those trees who're alive," Leigh shouted.

The guerrillas ignored her.

"We've got to help them," Leigh yelled even louder.

The guerrillas paid no attention. Damn the insensitive bastards.

Hours later, when calm had settled over the river, Leigh vented her anger at Paulita. "How the hell do you expect to win a war if you don't help people in trouble?"

"Why are you so hot and bothered?"

"I care about people in trouble and so should you. You can't let them drift by without lifting a finger."

"I won't do anything that'll endanger my mission. We can't help everyone just because they need it."

"Why not? You know what happened in Vietnam?"

"What does that have to do with it?"

"More than you realize. When Viet Cong insurgents refused aid to locals, they favored a corrupt Saigon government. Some day you're going to need help as much as these poor people need it now."

"I don't buy that."

"You will. You're against Marcos. If you're not Communists, prove it. Show the villagers how much you hate both groups, and the ugliness they stand for."

"You may have a point. Okay, we'll lend a hand if it doesn't delay us too much."

"What's the rush?"

"Soldiers will be on this river soon. With the low lands flooded, there's no way we can travel on foot until we reach high country."

Leigh cursed herself for getting angry. She would need an ally in Morales' camp if she had a chance of getting him to rescue Virgil. Paulita could have helped. Now she must make him understand he owed her for bringing medical supplies through a typhoon. It was a damn good reason, but would the guerrilla leader agree?

"Come alongside that tree, but don't let it bash a hole in the side of this tub," Paulita shouted. "Leigh, grab the baby from that woman."

Leigh ran to the side of the launch. Two men with poles snagged the tree, moved it toward them. Paulita shut down the engine to prevent branches tangling in the propeller. The roaring current carried launch and tree downstream together. Leigh lifted the baby out of the woman's arms as guerrillas pulled the mother aboard. Others shoved the tree away. A guerrilla re-started the engine, then headed against the current once more. Comforting the fussing infant, Leigh squatted next to Paulita who kneeled over the woman.

"I am Amy Baca," the woman gasped. "Take my baby to relatives in my village."

"Where is your village?"

"Valley below San Carlos Ridge."

"The river likely washed the village away," Paulita said.

"People will be on the Ridge."

The woman shuddered, then closed her eyes. Leigh checked for a pulse, shook her head. They crossed themselves, stood up. Paulita nodded. Her men threw the body overboard.

Leigh sighed, accepting the quick at-sea burial as necessary. She turned her attention back to the infant. "Poor little thing is suffering from hunger and exposure."

She went to the hold, took off the baby's wet garments, shaking her head at scratches and bruises covering the little girl's body. Leigh wrapped the baby in a dry towel, placed her on a bunk and covered her with a blanket. Finding milk in the refrigerator, she poured it into a pan and heated it on a hot plate. Then she rummaged through medical supplies for a rubber glove, poured warm milk in it and pricked a hole in a finger. Leigh lifted and cradled the baby.

"Okay, little girl, drink it all."

The baby drank the milk, then fell asleep. Cuddling the child in her arms, Leigh walked back and forth, singing softly as a warm glow enveloped her. It reminded her of her own child, her lost son. Oh Lord, where was he? She sighed again. First, she must rescue Virgil. Maybe she could take care of this little one too.

At dusk, the baby awoke and started fussing. Leigh went through the medical supplies again. Finding a non-aspirin pain reliever, she ground up a tablet, mixed part of it with milk. By dawn, the infant's temperature was down.

Paulita entered the cabin. "My God, Leigh. What have you done to the supplies?"

"Sorry, Paulita. I was looking for something to bring the baby's temperature down. She'll be all right now."

"We're coming to San Carlos Ridge. This is the place where the mother told us to bring the baby."

Leigh followed Paulita up on deck, spotting a group of people huddled together above the swollen river. Though she wanted to care for the child permanently, Leigh realized it would be better off with family.

"We're looking for relatives of Amy Baca," Paulita said as her men tied up to a tree.

"I am Amy's father. She and her child were washed away by the flood, but we could do nothing to save them."

"This is your granddaughter," Leigh said. "We managed to pull her out of the river. I'm sorry, but your daughter didn't survive."

Leigh stepped off the boat, handed the baby to the old man. She returned to the hold, selected medical supplies, then put them in a bag and went ashore again.

"You'll need the water purification tablets and medicine in this bag," she said to the elder. "There's enough for you and survivors from nearby villages if you'll share."

"Where are you from and what is your name? We want to thank you properly when our grief has faded."

"The medicine is from Miguel Morales, who suffers with you in your time of sorrow."

Leigh returned to the boat and huddled in the hold, waiting until they got under way. Then she went out on deck, realizing there was no better time to face Paulita's wrath.

"If I hadn't seen some truth in what you said, I'd have taken those supplies away from them," Paulita said. "You've got to face Miguel, but I'll back you up."

A half-hour later, they rounded a bend in the river and came upon a military patrol boat. Leigh yelled a warning.

Paulita turned toward shore as bullets whined overhead.

"Leigh, take the wheel," Paulita yelled.

When Paulita jumped down to the main deck, Leigh climbed the ladder.

"On my orders," Paulita said. "Ready—aim—fire. Okay, again. Ready—aim—fire."

The patrol boat backed away from the concentrated barrage. Suddenly, a shell exploded behind the motor launch, another even closer. Another cannon joined the first, salvos exploding on both sides of the launch.

They were in range of the enemy's big guns.

Chapter XII

Leigh cringed as enemy gunners fired another salvo. One five inch shell exploded alongside Paulita's sixty-foot launch, sending up a geyser of water. Another smashed into the aft section of the re-inforced hull, the concussion knocking Leigh to the deck. She strug-gled onto her feet. The engine was misfiring, and they were out of control. The boat was also taking on water. She must jump into the swollen river and pray she could make it to shore. Leigh hurried down the ladder to the main deck. Spotting a tree—carried down-stream by the raging current—headed toward the patrol boat, she hesitated. Dare she wait any longer? The next salvo would come any moment. The floating battering ram smashed into the pursuing boat, sending gunners overboard.

Leigh was elated, but realized they had to escape before rein-forcements arrived. How? The guerrillas' motor launch was dis-abled. Leigh suddenly recalled a military training film she had seen about air/sea rescue operations. An idea flashed into her mind.

"I'll rig up a rudder, Paulita," Leigh yelled. "Do something about the engine."

"Get on it, Max," Paulita ordered. "The rest of you plug holes and bail water. Head for a tributary up-stream on the right, Leigh, and pray Max can keep the engine running."

Leigh ripped a piece of siding off the cabin wall, tied it to a pole. She went aft, cradled one end in a jagged hole on the damaged stern and the other in the water. Steering the big launch with a make-shift rudder took all her strength and agility to overcome the swift current. Still, they made progress toward the tributary.

"Paulita, can you go forward and guide me?"

"Okay. Stay with it, guys."

The crew stuffed bedding into holes and bailed water to keep the launch afloat. Max struggled with the engine, inching steadily up-stream. Reaching a narrow waterway, Leigh sailed into calm water to a sheer cliff. Paulita switched on an electric lantern, guided her into an opening in the face of the mountain, then through a tunnel into a cavern. The engine gave a gasp and stopped. The launch coasted to a dock. Men jumped off and tied up. Leigh dropped her rudder, sat down on the stern.

She sighed. "Now what, Paulita?"

The guerrilla leader went to the hold, tossed out packs. Leigh put one on, followed the others into a tunnel in a wall opposite the waterway entrance. They hiked through a damp corridor to a dead-end. Paulita climbed a ladder, stepped out and waited for the others, then sloshed along a muddy trail. Leigh lost her footing and fell. Covered with wet mud, she jumped up, hurried to catch up. Coming to a thick forest that protected them from the downpour, they trudged up one slope, down another, until every muscle in Leigh's body cried out for relief.

"How about a break, Paulita?"

The guerrilla leader ignored her. Leigh plunged ahead, muscles afire, lungs screaming. She had thought she was in good physical condition. She had, however, never experienced anything as demanding as this. Leigh staggered, slumped against a tree uprooted by lightning during a thunderstorm.

"Take ten," Paulita shouted.

Leigh took out her canteen, drank between gasps, then put her head against the tree and dozed. Paulita shook her. Leigh groaned, stretching to shake off stiffness, massaging cramps in her calves.

"Think you can make it now, Leigh?"

"Damned right I can make it."

"Eat and drink something first. And keep up or soldiers will be breathing down our necks."

Leigh looked into the faces of the guerrillas. They too were weary. Paulita had pushed hard because of concern for their safety. Leigh washed down cold rice and dried meat with water. Joining the guerrillas on the trail, she pulled bananas off trees and ate them. The forest gave way to rice fields carved into tiers along slopes of the mountain. Farmers, clearing tree branches and debris, eyed them suspiciously. Leigh waved at the children, got hesitant smiles. An old man stepped out onto the trail.

"Soldiers are waiting in ambush ahead," he said. "You must go around the far side of the village."

"Why do you warn us, Old Man?" Paulita asked.

"My cousin sent word of your kindness in returning his orphaned grandchild."

"How many soldiers?"

"About twenty," the elder replied.

"If we use the other trail, they'll know you warned us."

"Yes, but I owe you a debt of gratitude."

"Any soldiers in your village?" Paulita asked.

"They know we're afraid of them and think we wouldn't dare disobey their orders," he said, shaking his head.

"Leigh, go with the elder and take the medical supplies. I have an idea how to get the troops to chase us without risking retribution on the villagers."

The insurgents took off back packs, removed personal items, stuffed them in their pockets, then trudged down the trail. Leigh picked up half the packs. The elder struggled with the others. As he led the way into the village, Leigh frowned. There was something familiar about him. They went into a wooden building beside a raging river. Only half the structure remained. The rest had been washed away by flood waters. She had seen this place before. The elder dropped the packs on a clean wooden floor. Boys and girls in white uniforms rushed up. Orderlies and nurses' aides? Yes, this was the remains of a hospital. Was it the one where she had given birth?

"We need medical supplies," the old man said. "Ours were lost in the storm."

"I'm a nurse, perhaps I can help. We have tablets for treating water. There's usually an outbreak of typhoid fever after a flood. Do you know how to use them?"

"I'm a doctor. So you're a nurse? I need help with a child. Both legs were crushed. I had given up hope of saving his life, but with proper medicines, he has a chance. Do you have any antibiotics? Can you administer anesthesia?" he asked again when Leigh nodded. "And monitor the patient's vital signs?"

"I've done it in emergencies. Where are the other doctors and nurses?"

"Soldiers took them away."

The elderly doctor led Leigh to a spotless cubicle. Orderlies and nurses' aides followed with back packs, taking out medical supplies and placing them with instruments on a tray beside the operating table.

"We'll scrub in the next room," he said. "The child is being prepared."

Hours later, Leigh stood on a side porch, smoking. She had tried to quit, but nerve-wracking events of the past week intensified an old craving. Savoring the cigarette, she watched the swift current carry trees and debris down-stream. The old man was a good doctor and, despite his age, had kept up with changes. This operation reminded Leigh of another like it in Vietnam.

As she thought about it, tears filled her eyes, rolled down her cheeks, mingling with sweat and blood covering her surgical gown. She sank slowly to her knees, covering her face with her hands. Long ago, a Vietnamese boy had lost both his legs after stepping on a land mine. And the doctors couldn't save his life. This Filipino boy, injured by the forces of nature, might make it. But the tragedy in

Vietnam still tore at her heart. She took a handkerchief from her pocket, wiped her eyes, then went back into the hospital.

The doctor, talking to a man and woman surrounded by children, turned and gave her a thumbs up. Leigh smiled, headed for his office. She yearned for sleep, but questions preyed on her mind. The doctor entered.

"What are the boy's chances of keeping his legs?" Leigh asked.

"I can't do any more than I have. The parents are too poor to send the child to Manila where he would have a good chance of recovery."

"I can get some money, if that's all they need. I couldn't let the little guy go through life without legs."

"Money isn't entirely the problem. He'll need a lengthy period of physical therapy and someone to care for him during recuperation."

"I can find some one if you'll make arrangements to have the boy moved to Manila."

"I'll see what his mother and father say, then get back to you," the doctor replied. "You're certain?"

"Yes. Now I have some questions about another matter. My name is Leighanne Lincoln Jackson."

"I'm Dr. Jose Zurate. I had a feeling something was on your mind. Please hurry, I must return to work."

Doctor Zurate! Leigh was overcome with euphoria. Yes, the doctor who had delivered her child. Could he recall anything about the birth or what happened afterward?

"I was a patient here some years ago, and..."

A young man ran into the hospital shouting, "Soldiers are coming, Doctor."

Leigh dashed to the window. Paulita and a guerrilla were assisting a wounded comrade under the watchful eyes of ten soldiers. The injured man was Max Garcia. Like the rest of his family, he, too, was about to be killed by Marcos' soldiers. Leigh glanced around for a hiding place, then shook her head. No chance of escaping out the front, and she couldn't swim the swift-flowing river. Leigh looked askance at Dr. Zurate.

"In the attic," he replied. "There's an opening in the ceiling of the supply room."

She would stay there until it was safe to come out. Maybe she could even rescue Paulita. Ten soldiers, but the doctor had said twenty. And where were the rest of Paulita's guerrillas? Had they run?

Leigh glanced out the window again. The soldiers were questioning villagers who pointed at the hospital. Leigh thought she recognized one of the soldiers. She eyed the others carefully, then smiled. This was what she had come to expect of Paulita. They were all guerrillas in disguise. Leigh went out to meet them.

Paulita spotted Leigh, glanced around, then returned her smile. "Okay, guys, let's get Max patched up."

"The village elder is a good doctor, Paulita, but Max will need a few days rest."

"Soldiers will be here in two hours. We've got to be out of here."

Paulita was right to stay only as long as necessary, but she should give the wounded man time to recover.

"We'll take care of him, Leigh," the doctor said. "Keep an eye on our little patient."

Leigh went to the ward where the boy was recovering. His legs had been encased in plaster-of-paris, then elevated on ropes attached to pulleys at the top of the bed frame. Pity tore at her heart as it always did for injured children. She moved closer, took his hand in hers and prayed the operation had saved his life and legs. Though he remained unconscious, Leigh fussed over him, taking his temperature, feeling his pulse, straightening the bed, repeating each step over and over. Loud voices erupted outside the hospital. She rushed out.

"Okay, let's go," Paulita said. "You ready, Max?"

"You can't take my patient out of the hospital now," Dr. Zurate yelled.

"I've got a better chance on the trail than I do here, Doc," Max replied, holding his side, stepping gingerly down each step.

"Leave his back-pack and let's move out," Paulita ordered.

"Dr. Zurate, I must talk to you," Leigh said, realizing it would be useless to argue with Paulita.

"Go with them and watch over my patient. Take the last of our plasma and pray you won't need more."

"I've got to ask you about..."

The doctor interrupted. "Get him safely to his camp, then come back."

Chapter XIII

Leigh stuffed the plasma in her back-pack and ran after the guerrillas. Paulita set a fast pace. Leigh cursed under her breath. Why was everyone in such a hurry? She would never learn anything about her son if things didn't stop getting in the way.

Despite the forced march, Max kept pace with the others. He hitched up his trousers with one hand, held his rib cage with the other. Uncomplaining, he struggled not to fall behind. Leigh worried he would lose too much blood if they continued at this blistering speed.

"Slow down, Paulita," she shouted.

Paulita ignored her. Leigh shook her head. If this trail wasn't so narrow, she would run ahead and shake some sense into that stubborn little woman. Her admiration for Max, however, increased. The Garcia family had raised a gutsy kid, but his determination could cause more problems than he realized.

Reaching Morales' camp at sundown, Leigh put Max to bed. Though exhausted, she gave him antibiotics, then changed his bloody dressing. He had stopped bleeding, but his face was pale. She set up transfusion equipment, gave him plasma.

As Leigh watched over her patient, lack of sleep took its toll. She dozed restlessly. Max's wound, the boy's crushed legs, and her tour of duty in Vietnam haunted her dreams. She awoke unrested. The sun was rising. She checked Max's temperature. Slightly above normal. His pulse was strong, and his face had regained some color. It was a miracle he was alive.

"You must be Superman, Max," she whispered. "You need sleep, so stay with it. If I didn't have business with Miguel, I'd go back to bed."

As she turned to leave, Max woke up. "Glad you came home, Leigh. Got to get something off my chest in case I don't make it."

"You'll pull through this with no more than a few aches and pains."

Max took a deep breath. "You gotta stop getting mad at Paulita. She watches over us like a mother hen, but this time she couldn't."

"She could have left you in the hospital."

"Soldiers woulda picked me up."

"She should have set a slower pace."

"Miguel needed her for a special operation."

"Okay, Max, I'll lighten up. Now get some sleep."

"Not yet." He gasped for breath. "Remember when you and my brother, Leon, went looking for Japanese gold?"

"Yes, I remember. He and I had some good times when we were growing up. Searching for hidden gold was one of the highlights of my childhood."

"After you left, Leon found it. That's why Marcos killed my family. Watch out, Leigh, you'll be next."

"Sorry about your family, Max."

"The sonnabitches can't get to the gold 'cause it's booby-trapped."

"Okay, now go back to sleep."

"I got around the booby-trap, and stumbled on a pile of gold so high it made my head swim."

"Have you told anyone else?"

"Didn't get a chance. When I got home my wife was sick, so I went after medicine. Marcos' bastards hit our place while I was gone."

How much of his story was true and how much was the raving of a man running a high fever? She reached over to feel his forehead. It was hot, but not that hot. Max closed his eyes and went to sleep.

Leigh shrugged, deciding to see Dr. Zurate as soon as she talked with Morales. She turned. The guerrilla leader stood behind her.

"Didn't hear you come in, Miguel. Let's go outside so we don't disturb Max. I have something important to discuss with you."

He led the way out of the hut, then stood facing her, arms folded across his chest.

"If you want me to rescue your nephew, forget it," Miguel said without waiting for her to speak.

"You owe me for bringing your medical supplies through that typhoon."

"You gave my water purification tablets to villagers. They have time to boil water, we don't."

Leigh opened her mouth to argue, then thought better of it. Her face flushed. She must cool her anger. There was one way she might break through Morales' resistance. Agree with him, or at least pretend to agree.

"That was a mistake. Now that I know, it won't happen again. Anyway, you got more supplies than usual. Your middle-man couldn't get his hands on anything."

"We would have gotten more if Paulita hadn't left Max's back pack at Dr. Zurate's."

"You're going to reap huge benefits from that gesture of kindness."

"How do you figure?" Miguel asked.

"One of the lessons learned in Vietnam is soldiers can survive critical wounds if they get quick medical attention. Max could have been on his feet in a few days if he had stayed in the hospital. It'll take a week, but he'll recover because he received timely medical care from a good doctor."

"What's your point?"

"You lose too many men because they don't get immediate medical attention."

"I suppose you know how to solve my problems?"

"The hospital where we left the medical supplies isn't close enough to your operations to eliminate all of them, but it offers a chance for some of your wounded."

Miguel put a hand to his chin. Perhaps she had been too blunt. He was young and had such an inflated ego he might get angry. No, he was intelligent and would recognize the truth in what she said.

Miguel twisted the ends of his shaggy mustache. "You've made a good argument for buttering-up the villagers. Okay, now I've got a deal for you. Treat my wounded, train my corpsmen and pick up medical supplies in Guam. In return, I'll rescue Virgil."

"I can't do that. I have urgent business with Dr. Zurate."

"Is your business more important than your nephew's life? I'm ready to launch an attack on a government facility, and I need you. Besides, I know where Virgil is being held."

Thank God, her nephew was alive. But he would be killed if he wasn't freed soon. Leigh realized she had no choice.

"Okay, you've got a deal. After this operation is over, I must get on with my business."

Miguel pointed to a back-pack. She picked up the pack, then joined a group of guerrillas hiking out of camp. Was this the special operation Max had mentioned? He may not have been hallucinating as much as she had thought. Perhaps his story about the gold was also true. She sighed. Well, the boy with the crushed legs would be ready to move as soon as she returned from Morales' operation.

She was about to get into a guerrilla war with Marcos' Army. Would this one turn out like Vietnam?

Chapter XIV

An endless column of guerrillas descended the mountain through thick forests on a narrow winding trail, Leigh among them. Heavy rains had brought freshness to the air. She breathed deeply, savoring the fragrance of flowers and mahogany trees. The forest gave way to groves of coconut, banana and nipa trees, tiered rice fields and huts on stilts.

The path widened. A runner rushed by, fell in beside Miguel. A moment later, he left. Another took his place, then a third. Messengers from other guerrilla leaders? Brushing the sweat from her brow, Leigh looked back at hundreds of insurgents.

"Where are we headed?" Leigh asked.

No one replied. Fuming silently, she took a deep breath to control her temper, gagging on the stale acrid odor of sweating bodies. As the grueling pace continued—forever it seemed—her anger turned to anguish. Just when she thought it would never end, they stopped for lunch. Leigh slumped against a tree, sipping water, eating sparingly. Minutes later—even before she could catch her breath—they were on the way again.

"My God!"

Leigh rose, plodded down the trail with the others until sun-down. When Miguel finally called a halt, she collapsed under a bush and closed her eyes. It was dark when she woke up. Leigh switched on her flashlight, found a stream and washed herself. Then she trudged to a camp fire and sat down beside Paulita.

"I was too tired to eat when we got here," Leigh said.

"Shh." Paulita pointed to Miguel who was conversing with another guerrilla leader.

Leigh took fish and rice from her back-pack, dumped them in a mess kit and set it near the fire to warm. She glanced around. Miguel sat to the right of Paulita. Oh Lord, Sumo was on the other side of the fire. He seemingly ignored her, but she sensed it was only a sham. Hatred would likely smolder within the big fat guerrilla for a long time. It had been a mistake to embarrass him in front of his men. Hey, he shouldn't be here. He was a spy. Would Morales believe her if she told him about the meeting between Sumo and General Navarro? Leigh shook her head. Better say nothing and keep her eyes open.

"One last time," Miguel said. "Jun attacks, then retreats to the south, drawing the Army out of town. That will be the key to our success."

"It may be the key to success, but I don't like waiting for Sumo to blow up the armory." A stocky young man got up from his perch on a fallen tree to fill a canteen cup with hot coffee simmering on the fire.

So Morales' guerrillas were going to blow up an armory? Leigh frowned. Was it the one in San Carlos?

Miguel twisted the ends of his mustache. "Revie moves into position near the warehouse west of town. When Jun attacks, Revie takes out the guards, grabs the supplies and heads into the hills."

"I know what I must do," a tall handsome mustached man replied, sipping hot coffee. "How about the rest of you? Don't screw up, especially you, Sumo."

"Don't worry about me," Sumo snarled. "Make sure your funeral starts at dawn, Miguel."

This operation sounded important, but was it as important as Virgil's rescue? Leigh nodded, conceding it probably would be if she wasn't worried about her nephew.

"I understand the need for precise timing, Sumo," Miguel snapped. "Most of my company will set up an ambush east of town.

The rest will be in the funeral procession. When the hearse gets to Army Headquarters, the armory better blow up."

Funeral procession? Leigh puzzled over what she was hearing. Was this the only way Miguel could pay his last respects to a fallen comrade?

"Use only the men you need to carry weapons and ammo into the hills, Sumo," Morales went on. "Half your company, and all of Jun's, must keep the army busy at least an hour. It'll take Revie that long to clean out the warehouse west of San Carlos. In the meantime, I'll free Virgil and lead the soldiers into the rising sun to our ambush."

Leigh's mind snapped to attention. So Morales' special operation was in her home town, and it included the rescue of her nephew. Should she try to get those papers she had left on the closet shelf in Rosa's house so she could question Virgil about them?

"You won't need me to tend to the wounded until this is over, Paulita. I have to go home to pick up some things," Leigh whispered.

"Stay with me," Paulita ordered. "We can't take any chances on a security leak."

"Keep your radios on," Morales continued. "If there are no questions, be in position by 0500 hours."

Leigh watched Sumo, Jun and Revie leave. Miguel nodded to three men who followed the guerrilla leaders. She wasn't the only one he didn't trust. Maybe Morales knew about Sumo meeting General Navarro. Still, the success of this mission depended on people who mistrusted each other. She shook her head. That wasn't a good sign.

Miguel's company put out fires, slung on bandoleers and packs, then picked up rifles, heavy weapons, and moved out.

"Why so soon?" Leigh asked.

"Never mind, stick with me," Paulita replied.

My God, didn't these people ever rest? They had been hiking all day with only a ten-minute lunch break and this short breather. How could they put up a decent fight against well-rested soldiers?

The life of her nephew depended on worn-out guerrillas. Leigh bit her lip nervously as they hiked down the trail. An hour later, Morales' company stopped, then split into four groups. Paulita led her platoon to a small church, leaving a dozen guerrillas to guard the perimeter. Leigh followed her inside.

"Don't take any chances," Paulita whispered, creeping into the nave.

Candles flickered beside the altar. Bright metal hinges glistened on a casket. A crucifix, a statue of the Virgin Mary with baby Jesus in her arms and figurines of early Christian leaders filled small recesses in the walls. Leigh crossed herself. After searching the church quietly, the guerrillas stretched out on wooden pews. Leigh lay down, but couldn't sleep. She got up, went forward to the railing and lit three candles. Clasping her hands together, she kneeled, praying for her son, the boy with the crushed legs and Virgil. Then she returned to a pew and dozed.

Shuffling feet woke her. Paulita was leaving the church with the second shift of guerrillas. Leigh glanced at her watch. Two o'clock in the morning. Paulita came back with the insurgents from the first guard shift.

"Get some rest," she told them.

Leigh was still awake two hours later when Paulita went out with the last group, returning minutes later with those who left earlier. These young men and women must be special to do what they did day after day and month after month, with no end in sight. What made them dedicate their lives to this struggle? Maybe she would try to get to know these kids when the operation was over, now that she had become one of them, though not by choice. Leigh finally dozed. It felt as if only a few moments had passed when Paulita shook her awake. Leigh rubbed the sleep from her eyes, yawned, then stretched, flexing arms and legs.

"Come with me," Paulita said.

Looking around, Leigh discovered the others gone. She grabbed her pack, grimacing, and followed Paulita into a room behind the altar. Camouflaged field uniforms were piled atop packs set against a wall beside rifles. Four female guerrillas, in bra and panties, sat around a mirror. Two wore dresses, and a third was applying a gummy make-up to the face of another.

"Stack your pack and fatigues with the others, then get cleaned up, Leigh."

Leigh took off her clothes and went to the bathroom. When she returned, the guerrillas were in disguise. Gray wigs on their heads, they were dressed in black dresses, wearing make-up that made their faces look wrinkled with age under black veils. Only hands, torn and calloused by hardships, identified them as young women. Paulita, disguised like the others, handed Leigh men's clothing.

"Get into these."

As Leigh dressed, Paulita glued a scraggly gray beard and mustache to Leigh's chin and upper lip, then put gummy make-up on her cheeks and forehead to give them the appearance of old age. Paulita started clipping Leigh's hair.

Leigh grabbed her arm. "What are you doing?"

"You've got to wear a wig, and it's too damn hot with all that hair."

Paulita pulled her arm away, finished shearing Leigh's hair. Then she plopped a gray wig over the shorn locks.

"Won't someone be suspicious if they see five old women and thirty old men, Paulita?"

"Only ten of my guys will be disguised as old men. Like you, they're too tall to be mistaken for women. The rest of them should look pretty much like us. They're risking their macho images because of the importance of this mission. Come on, girls, stow your equipment in the jeepneys and let's join the boys. Mass should start in five minutes."

When the equipment had been put aboard vehicles, they went into church through the front entrance. Except for the insurgents, disguised as old men and old women fanning themselves, it was nearly empty.

"Where's Miguel?" Leigh asked.

"Shh."

Late arrivals soon filled the nave. A small group of men, women and children entered and sat in the front row.

Family? Mass started thirty minutes late. As the ceremony dragged on, Leigh wrung her hands. Would the timetable be thrown off, resulting in failure? When the service ended, pallbearers carried the casket out and placed it in a hearse. Family members got in cars, neighbors climbed on horse-drawn wagons. The guerrillas entered four jeepneys, sitting face to face on bench seats running along each side.

"This ceremony is for my cousin," Paulita said to Leigh. "She was afraid to join the guerrillas. So she stayed in town to be safe, but it did her little good."

Leigh put her arm around Paulita's shoulders, then spotted six Jeeps, loaded with soldiers, speeding toward them. She jumped to her feet, hitting her head on the roof. Had the Mass been deliberately delayed so the soldiers could get there?

Chapter XV

"Sit down, Leigh," Paulita said. "That's Miguel and his men. They're dressed as soldiers, coming to escort the funeral procession."

"Oh." Cheeks flushed, smiling sheepishly, Leigh returned to her seat. This operation was planned better than she had thought. Still, something bothered her. Morales' men looked the part. They wouldn't attract attention. How about Paulita's guerrillas? Would anyone become suspicious when they broke away from the procession?

"We're late, but everything's going according to plan," Paulita continued. "Don't worry."

Still not reassured, Leigh clasped her trembling hands. Had Sumo betrayed them? Morales' man, who followed him, would know if he had met with General Navarro after the briefing for this operation. And he would tell Miguel, wouldn't he?

Two Jeeps stopped at the intersection of a street running in front of Army Headquarters. Disguised as soldiers, the guerrillas got out to direct traffic. Morales' Jeep broke away from the procession when it turned again. A Philippine Army sentry glanced at them.

The sentry's attention was diverted by an explosion to the south. The ground shook. Was that the armory blowing up? Yes, Sumo had come through. Maybe he was a double agent, pretending to spy for General Navarro while actually working for Miguel.

"You're a no-good bastard, Sumo, but maybe I was wrong about you being a spy," Leigh mumbled.

Paulita's jeepneys followed Morales onto Santee Street, then dispersed and stopped. The "old men" and "old women" got rifles out from under seats, hid them beneath their clothing and stepped down to the ground. Mortar and heavy weapons exploded in the distance. Jun's company attacking?

As Morales entered Army Headquarters, soldiers rushed out of nearby buildings. The officer with them ignored the old men and women standing beside jeepneys, picked up a field phone and stepped atop a bunker, raising binoculars toward the battle site. The wind blew his hat off. It was the officer who had beaten her. The urge to kill overwhelmed Leigh. No, she couldn't.

Gun shots erupted inside Army Headquarters. The officer switched his attention to the building.

"What happened, Miguel?" Paulita asked on a hand-held radio. As she listened to his response, her guerrillas got out their rifles.

"Get back in the jeepneys—you too, Leigh—and wait for orders," Paulita said.

When Morales appeared at the exit, soldiers opened fire. He retreated. Paulita tapped her driver on the shoulder, pointing to the doorway where Miguel had disappeared. As the jeepneys headed toward it, guerrillas opened fire, forcing soldiers to take cover. Tires squealed as the driver braked to a stop at the exit.

"Hurry, Miguel," Paulita shouted.

Morales ran out and hopped in front. Two guerrillas followed, carrying a man between them. It was Virgil. They tossed him in back, jumped on fenders as the jeepney burned rubber in the effort to get away. Soldiers blocked the perimeter road. The guerrilla vehicles headed toward the main road, across a field of bunkers filled with soldiers.

Leigh crawled to her nephew. "What's wrong, Virgil?" He didn't respond, staring glassy-eyed. She prodded him, then shook him. Still no response. What had those monsters done to her nephew?

As the jeepneys dodged the scattered bunkers, soldiers opened fire. Leigh cringed as bullets whined by her head. A guerrilla screamed, fell against her. She eased the dead man to the floor.

Gasping for breath, she felt as though a wet leather thong had tightened around her chest.

"Snap out of it, Leigh," Paulita shouted.

As her jeepney went by Lopez's bunker, he aimed at Leigh and fired. The bastard was trying to kill her. She grabbed a rifle, propped her elbows on the dead guerrilla. Ignoring the odor of torn human flesh and acrid gun powder, she aimed and fired. The wheels of the jeepney dropped into a hole. Missed, damn it, she thought. As her jeepney swerved onto the main road, Leigh squeezed the trigger, held it on automatic fire. Bullets kicked up dirt in front of Lopez. Adjusting her aim, she continued firing. Hot slugs tore his thighs and groin to shreds, scattering his flesh and bone splinters over the bunker.

"My God!" she cried. The enormity of taking a human life hit her like a pile driver. Lopez deserved to die for killing Rosa. What she had done, however, sickened her, and Leigh's stomach rebelled. She vomited over the railing.

"Hold your fire," Paulita ordered. "We're out of range. Damn it, now they're coming after us with high-speed armored cars. Where the hell did they get them?"

She grabbed a bandage from Leigh's medical kit, held it against a wound in a guerrilla's arm. "Get with it, Leigh."

Paulita was right. Leigh realized she must put aside the horror of having taken a human life. Wounded guerrillas were depending on her. She crawled over the dead man to two unconscious insurgents. One had been hit in the lower chest, the other was bleeding from a wound near his heart. Leigh set up transfusion equipment. It was the most difficult medical task she had ever performed, treating patients as the jeepney bounced over a road filled with ruts. She followed the action out of the corner of her eye. Gaining ground, the armored cars opened fire. Two trailing Jeeps, hit by heavy weapons fire, swerved off the road. They crashed into trees and caught fire. Men, thrown out, lay motionless. This was Sumo's fault. Damn it, she had been right. He was a spy.

Maybe they would reach the spot where Morales had set up an ambush before anyone else got hurt. Hey, didn't Miguel say he would lead the army into the sun to his ambush? Oh God, the sun was on her right. They were headed north.

"This is the wrong way, Paulita. We're supposed to be going east."

Now she remembered. Soldiers had blocked the road to the east. There would be no ambush.

Guerrilla jeepneys entered a grove of palm trees, armored cars closing into range, heavy weapons ready to fire.

Chapter XVI

The fleeing jeepneys bounced over the wash-board road through the grove of trees. Closing in, the armored cars opened fire. Leigh saw the muzzle flash of cannons before shells exploded alongside her vehicle. She cringed as dirt and rocks showered down.

"They're going to blast us to bits," Leigh shouted.

Another guerrilla was wounded by shrapnel. Leigh grabbed a bandage and treated the wound, unconsciously following the action. A land mine exploded beneath the armored car leading the chase. The other military vehicles couldn't get by. As they turned around, trees crashed to the ground behind them.

"We've got them," Paulita said.

Leigh looked up. What was happening? An automatic weapons barrage tore into the soldiers from both flanks.

"Someone's ambushing them, Paulita," Leigh said.

"Hell, I know that." Paulita tapped her driver on the shoulder. "Back up the jeepney. We can't let one soldier escape."

Moments later, her guerrillas joined the attack. Deadly cross-fire ripped the soldiers apart. As the smoke cleared, Miguel waved to the ambushers, and got back in his jeepney.

"Let's go," he ordered.

"Who set up the ambush?" Leigh asked, bandaging a flesh wound on Paulita's forearm.

"The rest of Miguel's company."

"How did they get here so fast?"

"They've been here all along. Miguel briefed guerrilla leaders the ambush would be east of town, then changed it in case of a security leak."

"I hate to admit it, but I'm glad he doesn't trust anyone," Leigh said. "Guess he knows Sumo is a spy."

The jeepneys turned onto a road leading to a farm house in a clearing. Medical corpsmen rushed out, carried Virgil and the critically wounded inside.

"Start transfusions on these two," Leigh ordered. "I gave them all the plasma I had. They're barely alive."

Leigh had little hope of them surviving without a highly trained medical team. A whirling noise made her forget everything else. Helicopters? Lord, how she wished they were on call for med-evac as they had been in Vietnam. Leigh dashed to the window. Philippine Air Force gun ships. She looked at Paulita whose reply was drowned out by noise. The choppers moved to within a few meters of the house, hovering as if awaiting orders to fire.

Morales opened the door and ran toward them, shouting over his shoulder, "Leigh, you and the..."

"What'd you say?" Leigh yelled.

As the choppers settled to the ground, Miguel boarded the nearest one. What did that mean? Who cared, as long as their guns weren't aimed at her?

"Morales has friends in the Philippine Air Force who've come to pick up the wounded," Paulita said.

The medical corpsmen rushed Virgil and the critically wounded aboard. Leigh got on the chopper as Miguel jumped out. The helicopters lifted off, turned and climbed. Keeping patients alive was even more important now that there was a chance of their survival. But they had to get to a hospital quickly. Leigh went forward to discuss it with the pilot.

"That's right, Big Dog, the mechanized infantry unit drove right into an ambush," the pilot radioed. "We're trying to pick up the guerrillas' trail now."

Leigh stuck her head into the cockpit. Dan Hanks sat in the co-pilot's seat. Memories of their night together—when he held her battered body in his arms—revived her yearning for him.

"I might have known you'd be involved," she said. "Lord, I'm glad to see you, Dan."

"I knew you wouldn't stay away, but I wish you had picked a safer job. These helicopters are from our secret reserve force. I hadn't planned on using them except in emergencies, but I had no choice."

"My God, don't you consider this an emergency?"

"Didn't mean it that way, Leigh. I set them up when I learned you were on this operation. Just hope we haven't compromised our supporters in the Philippine Air Force."

"Thanks anyway, Dan. They scared hell out of me for a few moments. Where we headed?"

"To Dr. Zurate's hospital. We've started repairs, and have sent equipment and medics to assist him. Let's pray the word doesn't get back to Marcos."

"That's good news. It's touch and go for two of my patients, but they have a chance if we get there soon enough. That's more than I can say for Virgil."

"I'm sorry, Leigh. Government officials stonewalled Fred. He stuck out his neck to locate your nephew. He might even have disclosed his sympathies for anti-Marcos people."

"Will being here cause you trouble?"

"The Philippine government thinks I'm on a fact-finding trip for Congressman Williams."

"What am I going to do about getting a psychiatrist for Virgil? His mind is gone."

"We could fly him to Guam."

"That may be the way to handle it. I want to get Dr. Zurate's opinion first."

"We'll be at the hospital soon. The pilot will send false radio reports as though he's still looking for the guerrillas who attacked the

Philippine Army garrison in San Carlos and made off with your nephew."

"How will you get Virgil out of here if I accept your offer?"

"After they drop off the wounded, the choppers will look for Communist guerrillas. Two will return to home base, but our pilot will radio he's having engine trouble and is setting down to make repairs."

Minutes later, the helicopters landed alongside Dr. Zurate's hospital. After discharging passengers, two took off again. Orderlies moved the wounded inside where medics struggled to keep them alive. One died, the others clung to life.

When quiet had settled over the hospital, Leigh looked in on the boy with the crushed legs. He was sleeping. She studied his chart, nodded approval, then crept out of the ward, dragging her weary body to intensive care. Leigh waited for Dr. Zurate to finish examining Virgil.

"Get some rest, Leigh," the doctor said. "I'll see you first thing in the morning." He lay down on a cot and slept.

Leigh sighed, trudged to her room. Dan was waiting. She went into his arms.

"You must come with us, Leigh. I convinced the pilot to stay overnight."

"I'll think about it after I get some sleep, Dan."

"I know you're tired, but..."

She didn't let him finish, her lips meeting his and lingering. Passion mounting, Leigh's thoughts of the boy with the crushed legs, the well-being of her nephew, and the search for her son faded from her mind. She caressed Dan's neck and shoulders, moving against him, feeling the beckoning warmth of his body. They entered her room, arms around each other.

Chapter XVII

Leigh awoke before dawn. Not wanting to disturb Dan, she dressed in the dark, crept from the room and hurried to intensive care. Dr. Zurate was bending over Virgil.

"Damn butchers!"

"What's wrong, Doctor?"

He mumbled something under his breath, shaking his head. "Come to my office."

He led the way to a Spartan-like room. Open medical journals were strewn across a huge desk. Book shelves covered three walls. A hot plate sat atop a cabinet next to a sink and refrigerator.

"What's wrong with Virgil?" Leigh asked again.

"The pressure of what he endured was too much for his mind," the doctor said, wiping his glasses with a tissue. "Your nephew was tortured."

His words struck Leigh like a kick in the stomach. Head spinning, she went to a window overlooking the swollen river, held onto the sill.

Though she had suspected Virgil had been tortured, the doctor's confirmation infuriated her. She shook her head. This was no time for anger.

"I have to make a decision about Virgil's care," Leigh said. "What are his chances of recovery?"

"If your nephew recovers his mind, it may never be the same. Even more tragic, he won't walk again. A bullet is lodged near his spinal cord. It's too risky to remove."

Leigh brushed tears from her eyes as Dr. Zurate put his arms around her comfortingly. Virgil's mind gone, his legs paralyzed. The prognosis was worse than she had imagined.

"Leigh, I'm sorry, but I have pressing work," the doctor said. "The boy with the crushed legs is doing fine, but I have to make sure nothing goes wrong."

"Give me a moment," Leigh said. "Do you think I should send Virgil to a psychiatrist on Guam?"

"He would be better off in Manila. My son is a priest, but he's also a qualified psychiatrist with the medical staff at St. Andrew's Hospital."

"Is a religious atmosphere necessary?"

"If he comes back to reality, your nephew will learn that with proper medical treatment he might have been back on his feet in due time. Spiritual guidance will help him cope with being crippled the rest of his life."

"What are you saying?"

"Government doctors withheld medical treatment too long. Please, Leigh, I must get back to my patients."

He turned and hurried away. Confused, Leigh considered his explanation. It didn't wash. Government doctors waited too long? The bullet couldn't have moved into the nerve center if it wasn't there in the first place, unless... Oh, my God!

The answer dawned on Leigh as she recalled preoperative procedures for gun-shot wounds in the back. Dr. Zurate had avoided the truth. Virgil's crippling injury had resulted from being tortured before medical treatment. Damn, she had forgotten to ask him about her son. Leigh ran after Dr. Zurate, catching up at the nurses' station.

"I know this is a bad time, Doctor, but I need answers to some important questions."

The doctor shook his head, heaved a sigh. "Not now, Leigh, I have too much to do."

"It's about my son, not my nephew."

"Your son?"

"You were physician at his birth twenty-one years ago."

"I can't recall anything that long ago."

"Would hospital records have the information? My sister had Virgil at the same time."

"Records were washed away with the back part of the hospital. My head nurse would have remembered, but she and her husband—my administrator—were killed in a automobile accident several years ago. Why do you need to know?"

"My sister told me my son died at birth. Recently, she confessed that was a lie. I'm trying to find him."

"You thought your son was dead? Doesn't your sister know where he is?"

"She was killed by soldiers before I could confront her. She told me nothing on the telephone."

"If I had a look at the birth certificate, it might trigger my memory," the doctor said.

"Don't know if I can find it, but I can get Virgil's."

"Bring what you can. Now that I think about it, my hospital administrator took copies of medical records home. I admonished him, but he was my nephew and took advantage of our relationship. If you can get hold of them it may help."

"Did he and your head nurse have any children?"

"Two adopted daughters, one born about the time you mentioned, the other seven years later."

"Where do they live? What's their names?"

"Marcella and Christina Moreto. They live in San Carlos. Now I must get back to work."

Orderlies carried Virgil out and put him on a helicopter. Leigh followed, but only to talk to Dan who was already aboard. She couldn't help her nephew.

"Virgil needs good medical attention, which includes a psychiatrist, Dan. I must stay here and train Miguel's medics as I agreed."

"You don't owe him anything. Morales knew where your nephew was all along, but made no effort to rescue him."

"Please, Dan, get Virgil to St. Andrew's Hospital."

"Damn it, Leigh, you must come with us."

"I owe Miguel. I'll give him six months, if it doesn't interfere with my personal affairs."

"What am I going to do to keep you from getting killed?"

"Dr. Zurate's hospital will make it possible for Morales' wounded to survive if we get them here quickly. Can you put a helicopter on alert for med-evac?"

"It's going to be hell to pay if we compromise any of our supporters."

"Do you want to help or not?"

"Okay, damn it! I knew you'd stay no matter what I said. I'll see you on Guam when you pick up medical supplies. I should have details of the med-evac worked out by then."

She hugged him, then got out. Waving as the helicopter lifted off, she watched until it was a speck in the sky.

As Leigh turned to re-enter the hospital, a bullet whizzed by her head, fired by a wild-eyed soldier holding a smoking rifle.

Chapter XVIII

The gun wavered in the young soldier's hands. Was he just nervous, or was he one of those kill-crazed lunatics Virgil had written about? Leigh glanced around for a way to escape. Soldiers were everywhere. She dared not run. She must try to calm him.

"Take it easy, Soldier, I'm harmless," Leigh said.

His finger tightened on the trigger. No doubt about it, he was going to shoot. Knowing she must do something, Leigh zigzagged toward the wild-eyed soldier. He fired. A bullet whizzed by her cheek. She caught her breath. He fired again. A hot slug ripped through her shirt, burning the flesh over her ribs. She sucked in air through clenched teeth. Suddenly, Leigh whirled. She slammed a karate kick into his stomach. The soldier doubled over. She wrenched the rifle from his hands.

Something hit her on the back of the head. Blinding lights flashed. Her head spun. She dropped onto her knees. The soldier tried to take the rifle from her. Leigh fought with all her strength, struggling to her feet, shaking her head to clear it.

"Take her with us," someone ordered.

Realizing she was too dizzy to continue the fight, Leigh released her grip, praying the soldier would obey the order. No more shots. She expelled the air in her lungs. Someone stuck the barrel of a gun in her back. She raised her hands. The soldier pulled her arms down, tied them behind her back, then hit her in the stomach with his rifle.

Leigh gasped for breath as soldiers marched Dr. Zurate and his staff out of the hospital.

"Move 'em out," a sergeant bellowed.

The prisoners followed him, a scout hurrying to the front of the column, four soldiers falling in behind.

"Are you all right, Leigh?" Dr. Zurate asked.

"I will be as soon as I can breathe again."

"Quiet, or I'll have you shot," the commander yelled. "Sergeant, wait for us where this path intersects the trail to San Carlos."

Though still nauseated from the blow, Leigh worried about the boy with the crushed legs. She must get away, then return to care for him. Intelligence officers in Vietnam had said the best time to escape was right after capture.

The column passed by rice fields, entered a grove of coconut palm trees. Leigh heard automatic weapons fire behind them. Were Morales' guerrillas attacking soldiers who stayed in the village?

"I was afraid they'd do that," Dr. Zurate cried.

Why did the doctor fear Marcos' soldiers so much? He probably believed all the Communist propaganda put out by the media. Left-wing newspapers continuously accused them of killing innocent people without provocation. Besides, there were only a few shots. They could have been shooting pigs for dinner.

When they reached a clearing, Leigh looked back. Smoke filled the sky. The village was on fire. She stumbled into the sergeant in front. He whirled, raised his rifle as though to hit her.

"Can't you keep your hands off me?" Exposing gold-crowned teeth, he grinned, then turned back to the trail.

Leigh glanced over her shoulder. "Dr. Zurate, I hope nothing..." She bumped into the sergeant again.

He slammed the butt of his rifle into her solar plexus. "One more time and I'll stick it to you right here."

The blow knocked the air from her lungs. Struggling to breathe, Leigh finally managed several shallow breaths. Anger boiled inside her. She forced herself to calm down. Now she must free her hands. What hands? She couldn't even feel them. Sweat, seeping into the wound the soldier's bullet had seared along her side, brought a stinging pain. Mosquitoes buzzed around her head. She couldn't treat her injury, couldn't even swat the annoying devils.

Perspiration flowed freely down her arms. Her bonds slipped a fraction of an inch, then another and another. She clenched her teeth to choke off a scream as blood rushed into her hands. Soon the agony eased. She shrugged, felt the ropes slide. She shrugged again, then again. Loose ropes slid down into her hands.

Almost free. She dared not act hastily. Still she couldn't wait until the main force caught up. Should she garrote the sergeant and run? No, he would fight. That would give the scout a chance to shoot her.

What was that roaring sound? Rapids? Yes. The soldiers could out-run her, but if she could beat them to the river, they would have a hell of time catching her in the water.

"As soon as we reach the San Carlos trail," she mumbled.

"What did you say, Leigh?" Dr. Zurate asked.

Oh Lord, she had forgotten the doctor and his staff. She would find Morales and get him to rescue them. The column came out of the forest into a clearing. The main body of soldiers, now right behind, spread out across the field. Leigh spotted an outcropping of volcanic rock in the shape of a camel's hump. Sumo's camp was near. And the trail to San Carlos only a little farther. When they got there, she would kick the sergeant in the groin and run for the river. A rifle barrel jabbed her in the back.

"Don't try anything," a soldier snarled.

He tied her arms again. She should have run as soon as she was free. Next time—if there was a next time—she wouldn't wait. Escape would be more difficult the closer they got to San Carlos. Once there, it would be impossible. Maybe she should take out the soldier behind with a karate kick, then go after the sergeant. Could she maintain balance with her hands tied? She had done it in training, but that was make-believe. Leigh chewed her lip. It was daring, but if she didn't escape before sun down, they would gang up on her.

At the edge of the clearing, automatic weapons erupted from both flanks. The gold-toothed sergeant fell, clutching his chest. As bullets whined overhead, Leigh dropped to her knees. She looked at the other soldier. He too was dead. Could she get his knife? Leigh rolled onto her side, turning her back to the dead man. She grabbed his belt, slid the bayonet out of its scabbard. Her hands were so numb, she could barely hold it. Better use her feet.

She rolled onto her stomach, grasping the long knife between the heels of her boots. Curling her legs, she placed the cutting edge against the ropes around her wrists, sawing back and forth. Strands snapped. She tried to pull loose. No luck. As the battle raged, Leigh worked frantically. The shooting stopped. This was Sumo's territory. She wasn't going to stick around to find out who won. Yanking her arms loose, she got up. Someone prodded her in the back. Hope fading, Leigh raised her hands, turned slowly. Long black hair rolled into a bun, pinned at the back of her head, Paulita grinned.

"My God, it's good to see you, Paulita." Leigh grabbed her in a bear hug.

"Come on, Leigh, we've got to take Dr. Zurate back to his village before the army returns with reinforcements."

They covered the distance in thirty minutes. Though winded, Leigh realized she was getting used to running up and down hills, or concern for the boy with the crushed legs had spurred her on. As they neared the village, shots rang out.

"Our advance party is taking care of soldiers guarding the place," Paulita said.

Leigh followed Paulita out of the forest. They rushed along dikes to the village. It had been burned to the ground. The stench of smoldering flesh struck Leigh like a slap in the face. She put a handkerchief over her nose and mouth. Bodies were strewn everywhere. Men, women and children had been shot or chopped up with machetes and bayonets. Bamboo spears protruded from the swollen stomachs of pregnant females.

"How could they?" Leigh screamed.

She vomited, convulsions continuing endlessly. Finally, she placed a handkerchief over her nose and mouth, trudged to the hospital remains, the origin of the sickening odor. What was left of charred bodies lay in beds, her little boy among the victims. Tears streamed down Leigh's cheeks, anger blazing inside her. She wanted to catch the killers, hang them by their thumbs and strip the hide off their bodies.

Brushing away tears, she strode around the remains of the building. Medical equipment, taken from the hospital before it was torched, was stacked on the dock.

"Okay, bury the dead and let's get out of here," Morales ordered. "Paulita, you, Leigh and Dr. Zurate stay with the supplies until our boats arrive. Then load up and move out before the army returns."

"Sorry about your friends, Dr. Zurate," Leigh said, putting a hand on his shoulder.

"Leave me alone," he snapped.

Was he blaming the guerrillas for the massacre? Soldiers were responsible for this, Leigh wanted to scream, but bit her lip in silence.

When the boats arrived, they loaded equipment and got aboard. The first launch headed upstream with Leigh, Paulita and half the insurgents. The other guerrillas and Dr. Zurate and his staff were in the second boat.

"I was surprised you didn't go to Manila with Dan Hanks," Paulita said.

"How come you knew where to find me?"

"We overheard a chopper pilot's report and headed for the village to warn Dr. Zurate. Our transmitter was damaged during Virgil's rescue, so I couldn't call anyone."

"Wish you had arrived sooner. Damn, how I'd like to get my hands on the bastards who escaped your ambush."

"I know how you feel, but don't dwell on it. Talk about something else, or it'll tear you apart."

"Okay, let's get back to the ambush during Virgil's rescue. Why did Morales change it?"

"I told you he didn't trust the other guerrilla leaders."

"I warned you Sumo was an informer. What has Morales done about that?"

"Miguel wants to see if Sumo got away with enough weapons and ammo to make the rescue worth our losses. Sorry, Leigh, he thinks Virgil may have been the one who talked."

"You saw what they did to him. That wasn't because Virgil talked, it was because he didn't talk. I told you I saw Sumo with General Navarro?"

"Okay, I'll check it out with Miguel. Oh, for Christ's sake, here comes a patrol boat. Get below and don't do anything foolish. I know you'd like to slit their throats, but we can't afford trouble."

Leigh went below deck. She paced back and forth, then rummaged through lockers, finding an old rifle. The odor of human flesh and the charred body of her little boy clouded her mind. She hurried to an open port, seeing one patrol boat, though two more came around the bend behind the first. Resting the barrel of the rifle on the porthole, Leigh aimed at the helmsman and squeezed the trigger.

Chapter XIX

The hammer snapped into firing position, clicking on an empty chamber. No bullets. Leigh gnashed her teeth. Then she spotted two patrol boats behind the first. How had she missed them? She turned away from the porthole, leaned back against the bulkhead and slumped to the floor. Violence had stalked her again—as it had much of her life—and once more it had gotten the upper hand. Time she learned to cope.

"Get hold of yourself," Leigh scolded aloud.

She hurried to the locker and stashed the gun. After splashing cold water on her face, Leigh went on deck. The patrol boats were headed down-stream.

Paulita scowled. "I suppose you found the gun?"

"You knew there were no bullets in it."

"I'm not stupid enough to give you a loaded gun the way you feel. Be patient, Leigh, your time will come."

"I'm beginning to get the point, but patience is not my strong suit. Teach me how to use that rifle."

"You may need to know in an emergency, but that M-1 is too heavy. Come with me."

Paulita turned the helm over to a companion and took Leigh below deck. She opened a hidden compartment behind a locker and took out a new rifle.

"This is an Armelite. Almost identical to the U.S. military M-16, but it's been modified to fully automatic."

Paulita tossed the rifle in the air, caught it to demonstrate its light weight. She disassembled the gun, placing parts carefully on the table.

"This is the barrel," Paulita said, picking up a long slender cylinder.

Everyone knew that. Well, if starting from scratch was what it took, Leigh would keep her mouth shut.

Holding the barrel, Paulita picked up the stock. She put the rifle together, naming each piece.

"Now you do it, Leigh."

Leigh remembered the barrel and the trigger, nothing else. She forgot where the pieces fit as soon as she removed them from the rifle.

Paulita shook her head. "Pay attention."

Leigh realized her concentration was lacking. She must forget her son, and the boy with the crushed legs. Okay, she would listen carefully to instructions.

An hour later, Paulita glanced at her watch. "That's enough. You've got the general idea. Keep at it until you can do it blind-folded."

"I thought my Daddy was joking when he told me about taking his old Springfield apart in the dark. Anyway, why do I have to learn so much just to shoot?"

"Guns jam, and if it happens at night, you're in real trouble unless you know everything about the one you're using. I've got to go back to work."

Leigh went over what she had learned until darkness blanketed the river. She stood up and stretched, then struck a match to light the lantern. She changed her mind, blew it out. Blind-folded, Paulita had said. Okay, she would do it again without light.

"I have nothing better to do except sleep."

Leigh took the rifle apart, setting the pieces next to each other. Identifying them was difficult in the dark, even after repeating the names. When all gun parts sat on the table, she started assembling it, fumbling for each piece, then putting them in position. When finished, she was proud of herself until she checked the luminous dial on her watch. It had taken too long. Do it again. A half-hour later, Leigh put the last piece in place. Still too much time. Her stomach growled. Ignoring hunger, Leigh rolled her shoulders to ease aching muscles. She took the rifle apart, put it together, then repeated the procedure once more.

"Fifteen minutes."

Better, but not good enough. She continued until her head dropped onto gun parts atop the table.

"Leigh," Paulita shouted.

Leigh's head snapped up. She yawned, raised a hand to shield her eyes from the rising sun. Closing them, Leigh quickly assembled the rifle and handed it to Paulita.

"Looks like you've done your homework. Eat something and stretch your legs. We're almost at camp."

Minutes later, they pulled up to a dock. Leigh helped unload equipment and supplies, carrying them to a hospital under construction in the village near Morales' camp. Dr. Zurate didn't want her services as a nurse. "Stay with your friends," he had said.

Over his depression, he no longer blamed Leigh and the guerrillas for the deaths of the villagers. His new staff of skilled nurses and interns was ready to care for patients. While visiting Max Garcia, the gutsy guerrilla who had been seriously wounded, Leigh tried to get Dr. Zurate to open up. He brushed her off. He couldn't, or wouldn't, help find her son. The papers on the closet shelf in Rosa's bedroom were her last hope. She went to see Morales.

"I have personal business in San Carlos."

"My medical corpsmen still need training. Stop off on your next trip to Guam."

"Damn it, Miguel, I'm looking for my son. I have to get some important papers I left at home."

"You can't leave until my people are better prepared. Paulita says you're an expert in karate. When you're not tied up with the corpsmen, you can teach my guerrillas the martial arts."

He hadn't seemed surprised when she mentioned her son. He had even acted as if he knew about her search. Was he holding back information?

"Do you know anything about my boy?"

"I'll tell you after you get back from Guam."

Miguel hurried away. Damn him. She had volunteered to train his corpsmen, now she was his prisoner. Did he really know something, or was he bluffing? Maybe she should tell him to get lost. No. If Morales knew anything, she wouldn't get it unless she did as he ordered.

Leigh fumed silently, learning jungle warfare even as she taught medicine and karate. Max, now recovered, joined her karate class when released from the hospital. He worked at conditioning exercises with determination.

"Take it easy, Max," Leigh scolded.

"It's gonna take time to get my strength back, Leigh. I gotta push hard."

"Marcos will be around next month, and next year too."

Max grinned, ran a hand through his short-cropped hair. He slowed his effort a few moments, then continued with reckless abandon.

Morales called Leigh to his hut the night before she was to leave for Guam.

"I'm sending Roberto with you," he said. "He'll take over the medical resupply after this trip. Then you can get on with the search for your son."

"I have a feeling you know something."

"We'll talk about it later. Pick up a Philippine Army uniform from the supply hut, and a make-up kit to disguise yourself as a soldier."

"Paulita says Virgil's mental condition has improved. I should go to Manila to see him after I get back from Guam."

"You can go with me next month."

"What happens in August?" Leigh asked.

"Never mind. Get ready for your trip."

Shortly after sunset next day, Leigh, Paulita and Roberto reached the outskirts of San Carlos after a two-hour hike. Roberto changed into an Army uniform and left.

"You can go home and pick up your papers, Leigh, but get to the bus station on time," Paulita said.

"You're not going with me?"

"I have other business. Remember, the bus leaves at midnight."

Leigh washed herself in a stream, then put on an Army uniform. Using a flashlight and hand-held mirror, she glued a mustache to her upper lip, and frowned. The jungle was playing hell with her skin. Leigh rubbed a cosmetic on her face to darken her complexion. She slung on her pack and hiked to the cane field back of her family home. Was that a candle flickering in an upstairs room? Maybe General Navarro had left a soldier on guard. Leigh waited, watching and listening for activity inside the house.

Seeing and hearing nothing the next hour, she finally entered her home, crept through the kitchen and dining room, then up the stairs to the master bedroom. Going to the closet, she shined a flashlight on the shelf. The papers were gone. Leigh swept the sweaters onto the floor to be certain they weren't hidden between them. Shaking her head, she dropped to her knees, crawled to the safe, then opened it and rifled through documents. Nothing useful. Did the maid know anything?

"Marci might have taken them," she said aloud.

A light shined into the closet. "What do you want with Marci?" a frightened voice asked.

Leigh crawled out. A girl, about fourteen, dressed in a long white nightgown, was holding a shotgun and flashlight.

"I'm friendly," Leigh said. "Put the gun down. Do you know where I can find Marci?"

"You're a girl."

"Yes, but who are you?"

"I'm Tina, Marci's sister."

"Where is she?"

"In Manila taking care of Virgil. Are you Leigh?"

"Yes. I'm looking for some papers I left here."

"Marci said to tell you Sumo stole the diaries. She took the other things to Manila to keep them safe. I'm supposed to stay here until you come. May I go home now?"

"I better go with you. No telling who might be out at this time of night."

Had Marci meant Sumo had taken Rosa's household ledgers when she said diaries? Why would he want them? More important, how would Leigh get them back? Could she convince Miguel to help her if she bought extra medical supplies with her own money?

"Get dressed, Tina, we've got to hurry."

As they strode toward the girl's home, Leigh realized she had cut the time too close. As they hurried along an unlighted street, footsteps clomped behind them.

"Someone's following us, Leigh."

Chapter XX

The shadowy figures behind them closed in. Leigh and Tina jogged to the girl's house. Leigh waited at the gate until she was inside, then ran to the bus station. Gasping for breath, she watched the entrance. The pursuers entered: Paulita and Roberto, the guerrilla Morales had assigned to take over the medical resupply.

"Get on the bus, Roberto," Paulita said. "I'll take care of this."

"What's going on, Paulita?" Leigh asked. "You two scared the life out of me."

"Miguel told Roberto not to let you out of his sight. I convinced the temperamental kid I'd keep an eye on you while he visited his parents. When I showed up alone, he thought you'd skipped out."

"He looked angry when he got on the bus."

"He has a short temper, and can handle a switch blade like 'Mac the Knife.' Anyway, Roberto insisted on looking for you, so I went along to cool him off."

"Thanks, Paulita."

"Get on the bus, Leigh, but don't turn your back on that hot-head."

As the bus drove out of the depot, Leigh strode along the aisle and sat down behind Roberto. She had too much on her mind to worry about him. First, she must find a way to convince Miguel to get Rosa's ledgers. Then she had to locate the adopted daughters of Dr. Zurate's former head nurse and administrator. Hey, Moreto was the name on the mailbox at the girl's house. The doctor had said Marcella and Christina Moreto, hadn't he? Yes, Marci and Tina.

The bus arrived in Lingayan at dawn. Leigh and Roberto found an overloaded jeepney, jumped on the rear step and hung on as it sped to the dock.

The crew of a deep-sea fishing boat cast off when they had boarded. The weather was fair, and the journey to Guam smooth, though uncomfortable with Roberto hovering over her. What did he think she was going to do, jump overboard and swim to shore?

Leigh hoped Dan hadn't forgotten his promise to meet her. If only they had more time to see each other. Even after vowing not to get involved again, she longed to be with him.

Tense and irritable when they docked at the Agana pier, Leigh cornered Roberto as she was leaving the boat.

"I'll meet you at the supplier's office in the morning, Roberto. Now get lost."

"Miguel said to watch you. And that's what I'm going to do, or he'll have my ass."

"Back off, or you'll lose something more valuable than your ass," Leigh said, eyes blazing.

"What do you mean?"

Leigh took her machete out of its scabbard and slapped the flat blade against the palm of her hand.

"If I catch you near me, you'd better be wearing a steel jock strap. Now do you understand?"

Roberto's face paled. Leigh stepped onto the dock, walked quickly toward the Toyota that had stopped. Dan got out, grabbed her and kissed her. Then he hustled Leigh into the car and drove away, a frown on his face. Was something wrong?

"I can't stay, Leigh," Dan said, brushing sandy hair from his eyes. "Congressman Williams is on his way back to the Philippines. His plane landed here for fuel. He expects me to go to Manila with him."

"Can you hold off until tomorrow?"

"I'm having trouble keeping him in the dark about my anti-Marcos friends. He's been talking about assigning a right-winger to work with me. If I'm not aboard his plane when it leaves, that's what he'll do."

Dan was going to leave without spending any time with her? Three weeks ago he had wanted to see her again as soon as possible. Now he didn't seem to care.

"But..."

"I'd be of no use to you if someone was looking over my shoulder, Leigh. Twenty minutes until take-off. I'd better cover procedures for calling an emergency chopper if you run into trouble. I've written some things in this notebook."

Leigh glanced at what he had jotted down. Frequency for radioing the chopper, secret call signs, little else.

"How about broadcasting in the clear, Dan?"

"That bothered me, but I think we can get around that if you'll transpose the numbers of the ground coordinates in your position report."

"Sounds okay. How do you want to do it?"

"Reverse the coordinates. Okay? Now a few things I didn't have time to include."

Dan finished talking as they pulled up in front of the air terminal. He kissed her, grabbed his bag and ran to the plane. Was he dumping her again?

Furious at Dan's sudden departure, she drove to Cathy's hotel.

"Come on, Leigh, we all have problems," Cathy reassured her. "Fred Skarlotta is having trouble keeping his work with our group from the Ambassador."

"Is there anything I can do to get Dan to spend a little more time with me?"

"You're pushing forty. Better start taking care of yourself. Tramping around that jungle is the pits, and lipstick isn't enough."

Leigh studied Cathy. Blonde hair, perfectly coiffed. Skin, flawless. Hands, smooth as satin. Nails, manicured. Lord, what she wouldn't give to look that good again.

"Come on, Cathy, that's not why Dan left in such a hurry, is it?"

"Probably not, but keep it in mind. And make the most of what little time you have together."

Chapter XXI

Cathy's advice on her mind, Leigh carried skin care creams to the Philippines when she delivered medical supplies to the guerrillas' camp. Anxious to retrieve her sister's ledgers, she asked Morales for help. He put her off.

"Damn it, Miguel, I used my own money to buy some of the medical supplies on this trip. You owe me."

"Something has come up," he replied. "I can't afford to send anyone to Sumo's village now. Later—maybe."

Leigh shook her head. "Okay, I'll head for San Carlos to check on the Moreto family."

"Not now, Leigh. Just be patient until I work out some problems."

Leigh stomped away. Morales was trying her patience. Well, she would slip out of camp when he wasn't looking. But that was impossible. Someone watched her every minute, day and night. Morales finally came to her nipa-hut.

"Sumo has gone into hiding. Probably suspects we're on to him. I'm sending Paulita to his village. You can go along and pick up your sister's diaries."

"I suppose that means I must accompany you to Manila for this chance at retrieving them?"

"You're beginning to catch on. You're going there to check on Virgil anyway. And you have to pick up the papers Marci took from your home for safe-keeping."

"Do you have any idea why Sumo wanted Rosa's ledgers?"

"Blackmail is one of his family's way of financing their activities. Your sister dug up a lot of dirt on everyone in San Carlos and wrote it down in her dairy."

"Paulita says Sumo's adopted family's name is Zurate. Any relation to Dr. Zurate?"

"Our doctor disowned them. Better get ready. Paulita is leaving in a few minutes."

Leigh put a medical kit and personal items into a back-pack, fastened a coil of rope and a machete to her waist, then joined Paulita. The pace was fast, and Max, who insisted on coming, had a hard time keeping up.

"What's the hurry, Paulita?" Leigh asked.

"We're going with you to Manila this afternoon."

"I'm not leaving until day after tomorrow."

"It's been pushed ahead."

"Why the hell didn't Miguel tell me? What about this patrol? I'm certain Morales didn't set it up so I can get my sister's ledgers."

"He thinks the village elder is a government spy. His contact in Manila is the elder's nephew. We'll check it out, then catch the bus in San Carlos this afternoon."

"Is Dan Hanks involved?"

"He sent Miguel a message saying Senator Aquino is returning to the Philippines from exile."

Leigh started to speak, then frowned, sniffed the air. Forest smells, sweating body odors and something else. Smoke from a campfire? Yes. On the other side of the clearing?

"I smell smoke, Paulita. This could be a trap."

"One of my scouts will call if anything is wrong."

Paulita started across the clearing, protected on the left flank by a solid rock wall leading to a plateau above the valley. The guerrillas, however, hunched down as they crossed a dry stream bed intersecting the clearing, unlocking safety catches on their rifles. The sun glistened off a metal object on the far side of the clearing.

"Hit the deck," Leigh yelled, diving into a trench, rifle falling off her shoulder.

The guerrillas dropped to the ground as a barrage of automatic weapons opened up from across the clearing. Leigh reached for her rifle, touched a sticky moisture on her pants leg. Had she been shot? She pulled up her trouser leg expecting to see blood. Her ankle was covered with a creamy substance. Leigh unzipped the calf-high pocket in her fatigues. A bullet had gone through the pocket, tearing the top off a tube of moisturizing cream. She threw it away, wiped her hand on the seat of her pants, then slung the rifle over her shoulder and slithered in knee-high grass to where Paulita had fallen. A pool of blood, and a path through the grass led Leigh to an old tree. Face pale, Paulita was trying to stem blood spurting from a gaping wound in her thigh. Leigh unslung the gun, took out her medical kit.

"I should have listened to you, Leigh. Well, now we know the elder is a spy."

"So you and Miguel have finally accepted my suspicions about Sumo?" Leigh placed a compress on the wound. "Hold this while I get a tourniquet. I don't like using it, but pressure alone isn't going to stop the bleeding."

"Sumo made off with so much ammo Miguel didn't think about anything else. Ouch, that hurts."

"Sorry. Why did you change your minds?"

"We realized Sumo couldn't have carted off that much in daylight unless the commander let him. Am I going to lose my leg?" Paulita crossed herself.

"No, but I've got to get you to a hospital. Can you crawl back to the dry stream bed we passed? We might have a chance if we can contact Miguel."

Leigh put the medical kit into her back-pack, slung the Armelites over her shoulder, then slithered to the dry wash, Paulita behind her. Max was waiting.

"Go get the others, Max, and follow us up this wash to the cliff on the left flank."

He hurried away. Leigh helped Paulita into the dry wash. She unloosened the tourniquet, then re-tightened it, wrapping another bandage on top of the bloody one. They started along the wash, the guerrillas behind them. Though Paulita's pace was slow, she continued until they reached the base of the cliff.

"We'll stay here," Leigh said, helping Paulita out of the dry stream bed. "I've got to change your bandages again."

Leigh dropped the Armelites on a boulder as Max and the guerrillas scurried to set up defensive positions. The enemy opened fire with automatic weapons and mortars, then charged. Leigh reached for her bayonet to cut off Paulita's bloody bandages.

Hearing foot-falls in the wash, Leigh spun around. Leading a half-dozen men, Sumo jumped out of the dry wash. Grinning maniacally, hatred blazing in his eyes, he raised his machete, rushed at her. My God, he was going to chop her up into bite-size pieces with that razor-sharp weapon.

Chapter XXII

Sumo almost on top of her, Leigh's breath quickened. Hand tightening on the handle of the bayonet, she pulled the heavy military knife from the boot scabbard and hurled it with all her strength. The blade sliced into Sumo's chest, burying itself in his rib cage. Eyes glazed, a look of disbelief on his face, he crashed into Leigh. His sharp machete sliced down her side. Her head slammed against a boulder. Air gushed from her lungs. Fireworks exploded in front of her eyes. She screamed a silent scream, falling face down in the sand.

Leigh struggled for breath, head spinning. She realized, however, she dare not pass out. Enemy guerrillas were attacking. She got on her feet, spitting out grits of sand. Whirling figures. Friend or foe? She staggered to the rifles. Bullets whistled around her. She grabbed an Armelite. Where was the enemy? As her vision cleared, she spotted the attackers lying in pools of blood.

"Thought Sumo was going to make mince-meat out of you, Leigh," Paulita said weakly. "Sorry I couldn't help."

"Yeah, we had our hands full," Max added.

Silence engulfed the battle field. Paulita's guerrillas had halted the assault. But the enemy would attack again. Leigh looked around to see how her companions had fared. Except for Max and Paulita, the others lay still, fatigues covered with blood. Leigh hurried to them, searching frantically for a beating pulse. Dead—every one dead.

Sweat, seeping into the cut in her side, brought a stinging pain. Leigh pulled aside a flap Sumo's machete had opened. Pangs of guilt enveloped her for thinking only of herself.

"Are you hurt, Max?"

"Nah, but you better have a look at Paulita."

Barely conscious, Paulita raised a hand for help, then closed her eyes. Blood soaked her pants leg from a flesh wound in her good leg.

"She's unconscious, Max. We've got to get her to a hospital. I better call for Dan's emergency helicopter."

"The radio ain't working down here in the valley. We got to get up on top of the cliff."

"How're we going to do that?"

"We can climb up that crack at the end of the wash. I'm still a little weak, Leigh. Will you carry Paulita? I'll be right behind you with the guns and ammo."

Max took out a red handkerchief and blew his nose. "Our guys put up a good fight."

"Sorry about your friends, Max, but let's get out of here before those bastards find out how bad off we are."

Flexing her knees, she squatted. Hoisting Paulita onto her shoulders, Leigh staggered through the wash to the fissure. Panting, she eased Paulita onto the bank. Looking up the fissure, she unfastened a coil of rope from her waist, attached one end to her belt, tossed the other to Max.

"Tie it around Paulita's chest while I climb." Leigh slung on her pack, tied two rifles to her waist. "Shove the radio in my pack, Max. I'll call for help when I get on the mesa before I pull Paulita up. How much time do we have?"

"They'll probably soften up the area a little longer with heavy weapons before attacking again. We might make it."

Leigh stepped into an irregular hole on one wall, put the other foot on the opposite side as shells exploded in the place they just left. She moved up with short quick steps. When the gap widened, she braced her back against one side, her feet on the other wall, inching upwards with both feet, then her shoulders. Reaching the top, she grabbed a tree, pulled herself onto the plateau.

"Miguel, this is Leigh, over," she gasped into the radio.

"What's your problem?" Morales asked moments later.

"We've been ambushed at Alpha Tango four-zero-two-five."

"How long can you hold out?"

"Thirty minutes—maybe."

"Better plan on an hour."

She sighed, wrapped the rope around the tree and pulled her wounded friend onto the mesa. Struggling for breath, Leigh untied Paulita, threw the rope down to Max.

Paulita opened her eyes. "Thanks, Leigh," she said, smiling weakly.

"Glad you're back with us, Paulita."

Mortar explosions in the valley stopped, automatic weapons fire increased.

"They're attacking again," Paulita said. "Lucky you got me up when you did. Max still down below?"

He was half-way up when the enemy opened fire. Bullets hit the wall alongside his leg, ricocheting into the sky. Leigh and Paulita returned fire. When the enemy ducked for cover, Max climbed the rope, scrambled onto the mesa.

"There's a trail on the other side that leads up from the valley," Max gasped.

Leigh ran across the table-land. Sumo's men were hiking up a winding trail. It would take them twenty minutes—maybe thirty—to reach the top. Leigh rushed back, took a pad from her pocket, grabbed the radio and changed frequency.

"Shell Game, this is Nightingale. Mayday at Tango Alpha five-two-zero-four."

She waited a moment, then repeated the transmission.

Agonizing seconds passed. Still no reply. Someone must be on duty. Dan wouldn't let her down. She called again.

"Nightingale, Shell Game is on the way," a voice finally answered.

A helicopter would arrive ahead of Miguel, but would it get there soon enough? Leigh shook her head.

"I left the guns and ammo on a ledge down there," Max said. "Didn't have the strength to climb with them on my back."

"We can't hold off an attack without more guns and ammo, Max. Any chance of going after the stuff?"

"I barely made it the first time, Leigh. It's taking longer than I thought to get my strength back."

"Okay, I'll go down after I start a transfusion on Paulita. Help me carry her over there."

They hurried across the plateau with Paulita. Leigh set up equipment as Max cut off a piece of rope and made her a rappelling harness. Leaving Paulita, they returned to the fissure.

"Give me good cover, Max."

"You'll get it."

Leigh stepped into the harness, fastened it around her waist, wrapped a rope over her leg, under her arm and through a loop. Max tied the other end to a tree. She peeked over the edge. No movement. The enemy had to be there. Maybe she could get the guns before they knew what was happening. She started down, rappelling slowly. As confidence returned, Leigh increased her pace, scraping an elbow on a projecting rock.

Gritting her teeth, Leigh continued. Reaching the ledge with the guns and ammunition, she slung a rifle over her shoulder, snapped a double clip of ammo into the breach, then put an extra clip in her breast pocket. She tied a rope around the other guns and ammunition. As Max pulled them up, the bundle snagged, showering rocks into the valley.

"They're hauling guns up on a rope," someone yelled.

Bullets whined up the shaft. Leigh tried to make a smaller target of her body, moving back against the wall, holding her breath. Max returned fire. The ledge seemed even narrower with bullets flying in both directions.

The shooting stopped suddenly. Had Max gotten everything up? She heard a noise below, but dared not step away from the wall to look. Was someone climbing the fissure? As she wrestled with her thoughts, a man's head appeared over the ledge. Leigh stepped forward, kicked him in the throat. He gurgled. Then his eyes rolled back into their sockets. He fell on his companions, knocking two to the ground, the others off balance. Leigh unslung her rifle, firing rapidly, bullets slamming into enemy bodies. As she bent over, staring in horror, the spare ammo clip fell out of her pocket. She grabbed. Missed it.

"Damn me."

Automatic weapons fire on top. Max and Paulita were under attack. They couldn't beat off an assault without help. How much ammo was left in the clip in the breach of her rifle? More than half full. Was it enough? Maybe Max and Paulita would be over-run before she got there. It might be a mistake to climb onto the mesa. She was safe here. She could even descend to the wash and escape. No. Her friends needed help. She climbed as fast as she could, joining them behind a large boulder across the mesa.

"How're you doing?"

"Can't hold out much longer," Paulita replied. "Miguel better get here soon."

Leigh peeked over the boulder. Three abreast, the enemy charged up the trail. She aimed, fired again and again. Click. Out of ammo. As Leigh looked for another clip, a bullet glanced off the boulder, hurling rock slivers into her face. Sucking in air through clenched teeth, she cupped her hands over injured eyes.

"My God, I can't see."

Grabbing a canteen, Leigh poured water into the injured eyes. The cool liquid brought some comfort. Blurred vision returned to the right one. She snatched a bandage from the medical kit, covered her left eye.

The shooting stopped. Leigh glanced around. Max, holding his rifle by the barrel like a baseball bat, said, "If I don't make it, Leigh, there's a map in my boot. It'll show you how to get to the Japanese gold buried on our farm. I wrote down how to get around the booby trap."

"If you don't make it, how am I going to make it?"

"Looks like this is it," Paulita said, taking out her bayonet.

Leigh grabbed her machete. Four armed men crept toward them. Should have escaped when she had the chance. Coming here hadn't saved Max and Paulita. Was it imagination, or did she hear a loud whirling sound and machine gun fire? Light-headed, Leigh took a deep breath, steeling herself for bullets that would surely slam into her body.

Chapter XXIII

Leigh felt her body for wounds. Nothing. Not a drop of blood. Was she dead? No. The injured eye and machete cut on her side still hurt. The enemy guerrillas, however, had been torn to shreds, their flesh and bones ripped apart by machine gun bullets and scattered across the battlefield. She shuddered. Overhead, hovering behind her, the whirling rotor blades of a helicopter—a Philippine Air Force gun ship—kicked up dust.

The chopper landed. Leigh and Max carried Paulita aboard. It took off. Fifteen minutes later, they arrived at Dr. Zurate's hospital. While Paulita was being cared for, Leigh showered in the nurses' quarters, then returned to the treatment room.

"You may regain some vision in your eye if it isn't exposed to sunlight," Dr. Zurate said.

"Did you save Paulita's leg?"

"Yes. Now get out of here, I have other work."

Shrugging, Leigh headed to the exit. Morales was waiting. He led her to the helicopter.

"I know you're beat, Leigh, but the chopper pilot will take us to Angeles City where you can catch a bus to Manila."

"Like this? I took a shower, but I had to get back into these bloody fatigues."

"Everything you need is in this bag. Clothing to disguise yourself, automatic pistol and bayonet. Even a make-up kit. Dan Hanks won't trust anyone else."

"You aren't going with me?"

131

"I'll be there tomorrow. I have to line up people to replace Paulita's squad, then spend the night briefing them. Coming in with new guys will put us in a bind, but we have no choice. I'll catch an early bus in the morning."

"Why do you want me to go now?"

"To pump Dan Hanks."

"You suspect him of plotting to kill Senator Aquino?"

"No, but despite his police training, Dan doesn't have a suspicious mind. He thinks Marcos won't harm the Senator."

"Why is Senator Aquino coming back to the Philippines?"

"He feels guilty about others taking the heat meant for him. And he thinks they'll only arrest him. It takes a son-of-a-bitch like me to recognize the situation for what it really is."

"What makes you think I won't run out on you? I've got other things to do."

"I've got your sister's diaries. I'll give them to you as soon as our mission with Senator Aquino is finished."

Her face flushed. She dared not cross Miguel or he would keep Rosa's ledgers.

"What do you want me to do? Ask questions and hope Dan comes up with answers?"

"Get him talking. If you don't learn anything, we'll be guessing where and how they'll go after Senator Aquino."

"Where will I meet you?"

"Outside the terminal, at Philippine Airlines. I'll bring name tags identifying us as baggage handlers."

"Will they attack Ninoy Aquino in the terminal?"

"Not likely, but who knows? We'll start at the baggage area, then join my people outside the terminal if everything looks okay inside. I need information, Leigh. Anything."

"No feminine garments in this bag. Guess that means I'm suppose to disguise myself as a man?"

"You'd attract too much attention if you didn't."

"All right, but I'm still a woman, and I'd like a little privacy to change."

Hours later, Leigh glanced at her reflection in a plate glass window of a dress shop. Thick eyebrows, bushy mustache. A black patch covered the bandage over her left eye. She had darkened her skin with cosmetics. Men didn't have honey-colored complexions, though hers had lost some of its luster. She could get by as a man if she controlled her voice. Leigh crossed her fingers, entered the Angeles City bus station.

"Last call. Bus leaving for Manila from Gate Two," the announcer bellowed over the public address system.

Leigh hurried to a bus filled with passengers, half of them off-duty soldiers. The loaded vehicle left the depot as she strode down the aisle. A young woman, sitting beside a sergeant, smiled flirtatiously. Leigh took the seat behind them, next to a sleeping soldier smelling of alcohol. Sighing, she closed her eyes.

Later, Leigh was awakened by the bus braking to a sudden stop. Yawning, she stretched to relieve aching muscles. The young woman in front stood up, then turned around and smiled at Leigh again. Scowling, the sergeant seated next to the woman pulled her down beside him.

The sergeant snarled, then kneeled on his seat facing Leigh. "Who are you staring at, One-Eyed Jack? Did you lose that eye peeking in bedroom windows?"

He grabbed the front of Leigh's jacket. That was it. She jumped to her feet, breaking his hold. Snatching the bayonet from her pack, Leigh grabbed a handful of his hair and stuck the tip of the blade into his nostril.

"A Commie took out my eye, so I cut off his balls," Leigh screeched. "Anything else bothering you?"

Oh Lord, she had forgotten to control her voice. Would anyone suspect she was a woman? The sergeant's face turned white. He nodded.

She sat down. Though the crimson hue faded from her face, Leigh's stomach churned. She should have held her temper. The sergeant, however, kept to himself, and the drunk looked out the window. Still uneasy, she got off when the bus reached the first stop in Metro-Manila. Standing up to the sergeant was stupid, but, Lord, it had felt good. She hailed a cab, then had the driver drop her at a department store two blocks short of her destination. As she strode along the street, Leigh looked back. Was the soldier ducking into that store her drunken seat mate? Imagination must be playing tricks on her. She entered the lobby of Dan's hotel, smiling in anticipation of being with him again.

When Dan didn't answer her knock, Leigh let herself in, discarded the disguise and took a leisurely bath. Recalling Cathy's warning about caring for her skin, she carefully applied cosmetics, slipped into a robe, thumbed through a magazine, then paced the floor. Footsteps approached the door. Dan came in. She ran to him, robe open in front, exposing the swell of her breasts. He gaped.

"For Christ's sake, what happened to you?"

"Just a sliver of rock in my eye."

She went into his arms. As she pressed her body against his, her hands glided across his back, onto his chest. She unbuttoned his shirt, slid it off his shoulders. He cupped her breasts, then moved his hands across her back and down, caressing her hips. Arm in arm, they rushed to the bed. Throwing off her robe, she lay back. He looked questioningly at the bandage covering the wound along her side.

"What happened?"

"Forget it, Dan."

"You're hurt. I can't forget it."

"Please, Dan, just for now."

"You sure?"

"Of course, I'm sure. It's only a shallow cut," she said, arms outstretched, beckoning.

Overcome with passion, Dan tore off his clothes and went to her.

Later, as they lay side by side, questions flooded into her mind. Why was Dan so quiet? Was it because of Senator Aquino's return, or had he met someone else?

"What's bothering you, Dan?"

"You told me the injury to your eye wasn't serious. Then I see a bandage that covers half your body. And you say it's only a shallow cut. I know you called for the Philippine Air Force emergency chopper. Was your situation that critical?"

"We were ambushed by another band of guerrillas."

"Oh for Christ's sake. Why the hell can't you get along with one another? Marcos is the bad guy. Remember?"

"I know, Dan. The bitter rivalry between guerrilla leaders gets to me. That's why Senator Aquino's safety is important. He's the only one who can unify opposing factions."

"I want you out of this mess. Why don't I throw in the towel on my job? Then we can go back to the States and get married. I took this assignment thinking Skarlotta would lead me to the bastard who killed my son, but he hasn't."

"I can't leave now, Dan. I must pick up some papers stolen from my home in San Carlos. They might help find my son. Miguel has some. Rosa's maid has the others."

"Where is she?"

"Here in Manila."

"You don't owe Morales anything. Chuck that job and get on with your search."

"Miguel is holding out until our mission with Senator Aquino is finished."

"Wish Senator Aquino wasn't coming home now," Dan said. "He can't do anything from a prison cell, and that's where Marcos will put him the minute he steps off the plane."

"Miguel says you don't think they'll kill him."

"Marcos couldn't do it even if he was stupid enough to try. Journalists with Aquino will see him leave the plane through the jet-way, escorted by police who go aboard to arrest him. Others will see him enter the terminal. The world will be watching through their eyes."

"Miguel thinks it's going to happen after he leaves the airport."

"If anyone goes after Aquino, it'll be another political enemy. Marcos will do anything to prevent it. Alive Senator Aquino is an annoyance. Dead he'd become a martyr."

"An annoyance? He's the only one who can unify the opposition, even from prison."

"You're probably right," Dan said. "Anyway, we must depend on him even though he did nothing during his previous confinement. But he's been away three years. People forget."

"You'll have someone covering Senator Ninoy, won't you? Where will they be?"

"On the plane, at the jet-way exit, everywhere in the terminal. Also along the route to Fort Bonifacio. Even inside prison. Hey, are you pumping me?"

"Of course." Leigh laughed, went into his arms, passion rekindling.

Someone knocked on the door to the sitting room.

"Who the hell could that be? My people know I'd have their ass if they disturbed me tonight."

"You told them I'd be here?"

"Yeah, that was a mistake."

Could she and Dan go out through the bedroom exit they had used when General Navarro's soldiers came after her? As they started toward it, someone banged on that door.

Chapter XXIV

Dan pulled the closet door open, pushed his clothes aside. "Get in here, Leigh."

She squeezed into the small space at the end. It was cramped and dark, the air stale. Sweat formed on her brow, rolled into her good eye. How long would she be here? Leigh put her ear against the wall, heard a garbled conversation between Dan and two men. Sounded like they were entering the suite. One voice was familiar.

"Come on out, Leigh," Dan said, opening the door.

Leigh stepped into the bedroom. The soldier who sat beside her on the bus—now dressed in a white seminarian's robe—stood behind her nephew in a wheel chair. The sparkle in Virgil's eyes showed he was back in the world of reality. The last time she had seen him, his heart beat and he breathed, but his mind was somewhere else. Virgil raised his hand in greeting. Leigh dropped to her knees, hugged and kissed him, then stroked his newly grown beard. She stood up, looked at the thin-faced seminarian.

"Auntie Leigh, this is Carl," Virgil said.

Leigh shook the young man's hand. He was handsome, despite a bald pate. On the bus, his military cap covered his head. Why had he been disguised as a soldier?

"You recognize me?" Carl asked. "I suppose you'd like to know why I was following you. I was only trying to make sure no one else had a tail on you."

"Whose idea was that?"

"Mine and Marci's," Virgil replied. "Carl told me you were fine in spite of your injuries. I came here because I had to see for myself.

From the looks of you, you didn't fare too well in your fight with Sumo."

Leigh gave his beard an affectionate tug. Dr. Zurate had been right. Treatment in a religious environment had brought her nephew's mind back more quickly than she had dreamed possible. Except for his paralyzed legs, Virgil was the same person he had been before being wounded.

"Okay, so I didn't come out of that fight unscathed, but I don't need a watch dog," Leigh replied in Tagalog.

"So Carl told me. I'd liked to have seen the sergeant's face when you stuck your bayonet up his nose."

"What are you talking about?" Dan interrupted.

"They're hungry, Dan. Come to think of it, so am I. You have something in the fridge, don't you?"

"I bought food yesterday. Let's go to the sitting room. Might as well be comfortable."

"I can't stay," Carl said. "My family is expecting me. Will you be all right, Virgil?"

"I'm fine. Marci will come by when she gets off work."

After he left, Leigh, Dan and Virgil ate dinner, then talked and drank coffee.

Virgil flexed his arms and grimaced. "They get numb sometimes. I'm still weak, but my strength is gradually returning. Auntie Leigh, you look beat. Why don't you go to bed?"

"I wanted to stay up to talk to Marci, but I can't keep my eyes open. Sorry. See you in the morning."

Sunlight, streaming through the windows, woke Leigh. She looked around. The apartment was empty. Dan had left a note on the refrigerator. He would see her after the panic in his office died down over Aquino's return. Marci had left a large envelope on the table. Leigh took it to the bedroom, looked at her watch. She would get dressed first. She removed a baggage handler's uniform from her pack, then a make-up kit, automatic pistol and bayonet. Rosary beads fell on the floor.

"Forgot I put these in here," Leigh mumbled.

She put them around her neck, hurriedly dressed, anxious to look at the papers. She poured the contents of the envelope on the carpet. Setting aside birth certificates, she went to her late brother-in-law's papers. His Philippine Scouts discharge showed Raul had been retired medically. She scanned the file. What had the doctor written? Raul's wounds had left him permanently impotent. She frowned. How could that be? Leigh ran her fingers over the words. Unbelievable. She dashed to the window, held the page up to the light. The original unaltered entry. No erasure marks.

"That can't be right."

Leigh read the entry again, checked the date, studied one page after another. No entries during Japanese occupation. The next one, in May 1945, was a physical examination. Raul was again diagnosed as impotent. It was confirmed with a final entry shortly before his death. Leigh slammed the folder shut.

"I don't understand," she said aloud. "Raul was impotent, physically incapable of raping me. Then who? Oh my God! It had to have been his half-brother, Fidel. No wonder Rosa was angry at me for accusing her husband."

Leigh realized that she was responsible for the rift with her sister. She had been certain Raul was the one. Until this moment, she hadn't considered anyone else. Now she knew the truth. General Fidel Navarro was the son-of-a-bitch who raped her. She buried her face in her hands and sobbed.

"Who's Virgil's father?" Leigh asked herself, wiping the tears from her eyes on her sleeve.

She looked at death certificates, finding one of a child stillborn to Leighanne Navarro, the surname she had used at Dr. Zurate's hospital. Rosa had said Leigh's son was alive, but the death certificate indicated he died at birth. Oh Lord, what really happened? Only God knew. An overwhelming urge to attend Catholic Mass washed over her. She checked her watch. Just time enough to walk to San Antonio Church for seven o'clock services, then catch a cab to the airport.

Leigh put everything back in the envelope, washed her face, fingered the eye patch, then completed her masculine disguise. She slipped a gun into the shoulder holster beneath her jacket, strapped the bayonet under her pants leg. As she put on her cap, Leigh shook her head. The first time she would hear Mass in years and she was going armed.

Chapter XXV

During her walk to church, Leigh became determined to clear her mind. She must concentrate on protecting Ninoy Aquino. Of all the things Dan had said, what was most important? The Senator would be covered by friends after he got off the China Airlines plane. And Marcos would increase security in the terminal. Anything else?

Mass had already begun when she entered the church. Initially, Leigh was engulfed in a feeling of serenity. It gave way to guilt for killing Lopez, Sumo, and Lord knows how many guerrillas. She grew uneasy, running out of church before Mass was finished. Dashing to the corner, she jumped in a cab, settled back in the seat for the ride to the airport. Again, she mulled over what Dan had said. Marcos would tighten security at the airport for Senator Aquino's arrival on China Airlines. Nothing more? She sighed. The cab pulled up to the curb at Philippine Airlines.

Morales met Leigh, handed her an identification tag. She pinned it on her jacket, followed him into the terminal.

They threaded their way through passengers carrying baggage, entering a room behind check-in counters.

"What did you learn, Leigh?"

"Dan realized I was pumping him, but he didn't hold back. I didn't learn anything important, but something has been nagging me. Maybe you'll pick it up."

Morales lit a cigar, rubbed the stubble of beard on his chin, then pushed the hair under his cap, twisted the ends of his mustache. Leigh went over her conversations with Dan. When she mentioned tighter security in the terminal, Miguel snapped his fingers, threw his cigar butt in the receptacle.

"Marcos won't wait until Senator Aquino leaves the terminal. It's buttoned down tight. That's because his people don't want anyone near him except their assassins."

"Where in the terminal?"

"Let's look around, concentrating on places with the greatest security."

"Someone might recognize you without a disguise, Miguel. I don't want to get picked up."

"I was all over the place before you arrived. No one paid any attention to me—or anyone for that matter."

"That's strange, isn't it?"

"They had something else on their minds. Now that I think about it, they took special pains to keep everyone off the flight line. Let's see if we can find a way to bypass metal detectors."

They hurried to an unmarked door. Miguel took out a bundle of keys, unlocked it. He and Leigh entered a long corridor housing a moving belt filled with suitcases, boxes and bags. They followed it to the rear where the luggage went out an opening onto the flight line. Baggage handlers put it on carts attached to a tug. The pungent odor of jet fuel and carbon-monoxide wafted across the tarmac.

"We'll wait until the baggage handlers leave, then slip out and check the flight line," Morales shouted over the whine from jet engines of a taxiing plane.

"We don't have much time, Miguel."

"There's no other way without passing through a metal detector, and I'm not going anywhere without my gun."

As they watched the baggage move by, Leigh rehashed her discussions with Dan. The flow continued for ten or fifteen minutes. Leigh grew angry at herself for not coming up with answers. What had she missed? Maybe Miguel was wrong in thinking Dan knew something. How about Aquino's flight? She looked at the mountain of boxes, suitcases and bags—even golf clubs—flowing along the belt. All had Philippines Airlines departure and destination tags.

"My God, we're at the wrong place!" Leigh exclaimed. "Ninoy's coming in on China Airlines."

"Are you certain?"

"Of course I'm certain."

"Dan's message said Aquino would be on a Philippine Airlines flight."

Was Dan involved in a conspiracy to kill the Senator? Couldn't be. But if he wasn't, why had he given Miguel false information?

"Come on, Leigh, up the stairway. We can get to China Airlines along the back of the terminal."

They went up a circular stairway to the second floor, stepped into an open corridor with large plate glass windows overlooking the flight line. On the opposite side, waiting rooms, without passengers, were sandwiched between walled areas. That figured. No witnesses. They ran along the row of windows, stopping in front of a door. Miguel searched for a key. Leigh watched the China Airline plane parked next to a jetway fifty yards ahead. Baggage carts sat between it and a black, white and yellow plane at the jetway. The area was cordoned off.

"Keep an eye out for anything that looks suspicious, Leigh. We don't have much time."

A dark blue van, "AVSECOM" on the side, was parked at the bottom of the metal stairway attached to the jetway near the connection to the plane. Several civilians stood behind the van. Was that Aquino's flight? The door at the top of the jetway opened. A man in a white safari suit started down the stairs, uniformed men holding each arm. Soldiers followed.

"There's Ninoy Aquino."

"Where?"

"Soldiers are escorting him down the stairs connected to the jetway."

"Damn, I was afraid we'd be too late," Miguel said.

A soldier behind Aquino took out a gun. Leigh tried to scream. It stuck in her throat. The soldier fired a shot into the back of the Senator's head. Blood, brain matter and flesh splattered down the stairs.

"They've killed him," Leigh gasped.

Soldiers dragged the Senator's body to the rear of the van, dropped it, arms out-stretched. The tarmac beneath his head and shoulders became saturated with blood. Suddenly, a soldier shot one of the civilians, then he and the others ran away. Leigh's breath became quick and shallow. Dizziness engulfed her. Darkness closed in. She grabbed the window ledge, breathed deeply. As her head cleared, Leigh's face flushed. Frustration and guilt seized her. As she stared at the horrifying—yet fascinating—sight, the rear doors of the blue van swung open. More soldiers jumped out, fired into the body next to the Senator. They placed a pistol in the dead man's hand, tossed Aquino in back of the van, then jumped in. It sped away.

"Someone spotted us, Leigh. Let's get out of here."

"Halt!" Security guards rushed at them, weapons drawn.

Miguel and Leigh ran to the door. "Cover me, while I find the damn key," Morales said.

Leigh realized she and Miguel—like the hapless civilian on the ramp—had been chosen as scapegoats—dead scapegoats.

She drew her gun, returning fire as police opened up. Bullets whizzed by her head. Others ricocheted off the concrete at her feet. Miguel groaned, slumped to the floor.

Chapter XXVI

Leigh fired quickly, four times, one after another, hitting a security guard. The others retreated. How bad was Miguel hurt? She glanced behind her. Morales had gotten on his feet. Bullets ricocheted off the wall. Leigh flinched, returned fire. The guards took cover.

"Broke off key, but door's unlocked," Miguel gasped.

Leigh pulled the door open, helped Miguel inside. The guards fired again. She slammed it shut, snapped the dead-bolt. Now she must keep Miguel from bleeding to death. Leigh took off her jacket, stuffed it under his shirt against the wound. Not a good dressing, but the best she could do for now. Hurried footsteps approached. She fired through the door, her bullets splintering it, heard a groan.

"Can you make it down the steps, Miguel?" Leigh asked.

"You go first. I'll hang onto your shoulder."

Leigh stepped down, Miguel behind her, descending to the first step, the next, then another. His legs folded. He fell on her. Hitting the concrete floor, Leigh heard a sickening wrenching sound as a sharp pain stabbed her ankle.

Sucking air in through clenched teeth, Leigh rolled out from under Morales. She must get away before guards arrived. Misty-eyed, she hobbled to the wall, flipped a switch, then dragged the unconscious guerrilla leader to the moving baggage conveyor. Shots rang out at the top of the stairs. They were shooting off the lock. She struggled getting Miguel onto the conveyor belt, then, breathing laboriously, collapsed on top of him.

Leigh took a deep breath, blew the air from her lungs. Whew. Unstrapping her belt, she wrapped it around her swelling ankle. Hearing pursuing guards, she snapped an empty clip out of her automatic pistol, installed a full one, then opened fire.

Reaching the baggage pick-up area, Leigh jumped off, pulling Morales onto the rail. Somehow, she must get him out of the terminal. She had carried her Daddy when he broke his hip, but she was much younger then. Now she was trained for this sort of thing. Could she do it with a sprained ankle? Leigh squatted. Grabbing hold of Miguel's jacket, she got her shoulders under his abdomen. Straightening up, she lifted him off the edge of the conveyor. Groaning under his weight, Leigh staggered to the exit. Guards came out of the corridor, but were blocked by passengers' baggage carts.

"Thank God for small favors," Leigh mumbled.

A cab was parked at the curb, engine running, rear door open. A chunky cabbie, with shaggy mustache, sat behind the wheel. He opened fire at the police. Leigh struggled on rubbery legs to his taxi, dumped Miguel onto the back seat, jumped in and plopped down beside him.

"Put your foot through the floor boards," she gasped.

The driver was already speeding away, tires squealing. Enemy bullets slammed into the cab. Red lights flashing, sirens blaring, police cars took up the chase. Three taxis pulled out in front of the pursuers. The cabbies jumped out, abandoning their vehicles. Guerrillas risking their lives so Leigh and Miguel could escape.

"Got a first aid kit?" Leigh asked.

The driver tossed her a medical kit. Leigh removed the bloody jacket covering Morales' injury. After treating his wound with antibiotics, she taped heavy compresses over it. Slumping back in the seat, Leigh sighed, then looked carefully at the driver. Of course, Max Garcia.

"I don't know how you knew, Max, but I'm glad you showed up when you did."

"Miguel set it up. Good thing too, even if we didn't expect so much trouble. How is he?"

"Lost a lot of blood. May have internal injuries. Get him to St. Andrew's as fast as you can."

"I used to drive a cab in Manila, so I know a short cut. Did they kill Ninoy?"

"Yes, Max, the cowards shot him."

Max grabbed a radio mic. "Lady Mercy, Max here. Miguel took a bullet in the chest. I'm bringing him in."

"We'll be ready," a voice replied.

Leigh checked Miguel's bandage. The wound had stopped bleeding. Maybe there were no internal injuries after all. Max drove through an open gate at St. Andrew's, then along a gravel roadway to the rear entrance. Orderlies carried Miguel into the clinic. Leaning on Max, Leigh followed.

"What is this place?" Leigh asked.

"Virgil convinced the seminary brothers to let him set up a medical refuge for guerrillas."

They took Miguel to the emergency operating room. Leigh sat on an examining table, unfastened the belt around her ankle, then removed her boot and sock. Lord, it was swollen. She lay back, closed her eyes. The activities of the day raced through her mind. Everything was piling up. Now the search for her son had to wait for Miguel to regain consciousness, if he ever did.

Chapter XXVII

When Leigh awoke, her ankle was bandaged, an ice pack wrapped loosely over it to control swelling. She sat up to listen to a newscaster on the radio.

"A former congressman was slain at the Manila International Airport this morning. Security police killed the assassin. His accomplices, however, who were wounded, escaped in heavy traffic. One has been identified as Miguel Morales, notorious Communist guerrilla leader. The other is unidentified. He's about five feet ten inches tall, with thick dark hair, eyebrows and mustache. He also wore a black patch over one eye. We now return to regular programing."

As music flowed from the radio, Leigh thought about the news report. The police didn't know who she was, but had a description of her disguised as a man. She must do something about that. The announcer identified the deceased only as a former congressman. Would Marcos let the media know of Senator Aquino's assassination? He had to tell the world sooner or later. And when he did, Marcos would blame the Communists. Filipinos and Americans would swallow his propaganda. If she hadn't witnessed the killing, she, too, might have believed it.

Virgil wheeled himself into the room, a canvas bag on his lap. "How are you, Auntie Leigh?"

"I'm not going to do any hiking for a few days."

"You've got to get out of that disguise. TV stations are carrying a picture of Miguel and an artist's sketch of you. You're wanted for questioning in the death of a security guard."

"I can't stay here, Virgil. The seminarians may be trustworthy, but I don't want to take any chances."

"If the doctor approves, we're taking Miguel to another place tonight. You can go with us, but Dan Hanks wants you to stay at his hotel until your ankle heals."

"Where is Dan?"

"He'll come by tonight to pick you up," Virgil replied.

"Unifying the opposition to Marcos is down the drain now, Virgil. After Ninoy's funeral, I'll get on with my personal business."

"Don't rule out anything, Auntie Leigh. The seminary brothers are against Marcos too, and we're only a small part of the religious faction opposed to his martial law."

"It'll take more than a bunch of religious zealots to force him out of office," Leigh replied. "Can you get me some dark glasses, a make-up kit and men's clothes?"

"Sun glasses and make-up kit are in this bag. I'll get the clothes while you do something about your appearance. There's a cane in the closet."

Virgil wheeled out of the room. Leigh hobbled to the closet, grabbed the cane, then limped to the bathroom with the make-up kit. After working on her face, she ended up with shaggy gray hair and beard, skin wrinkled to look like an old man. The black patch had to go. Keeping her injured eye closed, Leigh turned off the light, removed the patch and bandage beneath it, then put on sun glasses.

"Here you are," Virgil said, coming back into the room with men's clothing.

From the look on his face, Leigh knew he was satisfied with her disguise. She picked up the clothes, went back into the bathroom. When she came out, Leigh limped with the cane like an old man favoring aches and pains.

"How's the eye, Auntie Leigh?"

"I'll get by. I'm going to tell Miguel I'm finished with training his medics. Dan Hanks asked me to marry him, and I was thinking about it until the discrepancy in Ninoy's arrival gave me second thoughts."

"Keep an open mind, Auntie Leigh. Miguel has some ideas you may like. Hear him out before you make any decisions."

"I can't think of a reason to continue what I'm doing."

"And talk to Dan. I can't believe he'd do anything to harm Ninoy. But don't tell him your plans."

"I'll wait until after Ninoy's funeral, Virgil."

"Let's go see Miguel."

Leigh followed him down the hall into another room. Morales was sitting up in bed. His pale face was clean shaven, hair cut short. Despite his injury, he lit a cigar as Virgil went out into the hall and closed the door.

"Thanks for taking care of me this morning, Leigh. That was my only pleasant surprise all day."

"Glad I could help."

"I was going to release you from your promise to train my medics, but things have changed. With Senator Aquino dead, we're going to need you more than ever."

"You want me to stay on and nurse your rag-tag band of guerrillas?"

"For what it's worth, I'd have rescued Virgil without you agreeing to train my corpsmen. Dr. Zurate's hospital is near our base camp. I won't need you as a nurse, but as my lieutenant."

"What?"

"You're a born leader, Leigh. You instinctively know what to do in emergencies."

"Who will I lead?"

"Ninoy's death will bring recruits to our cause. We were looking to him to unify guerrilla leaders, but that wasn't God's will. We may never become unified, but we're bound to put our differences aside to overthrow Marcos."

"Since when do Communists recognize God?"

"I am not a Communist."

Well, she would let him think she believed him. If only Miguel really had a way to get rid of Marcos. Aquino's murder infuriated her. She wanted to strangle the real assassins.

"Okay, so you'll stop fighting among yourselves. But there's no way you can recruit enough people to bring down Marcos' government."

"Leigh, your disguise is good. You can go anywhere without being recognized. So go out into the streets. Listen to what people say. Not only will you be convinced our strength is certain to grow, you'll understand your role in the movement."

"I have personal business to attend to and I don't have time to check anything," Leigh replied.

"Take the time and I'll help you locate your son. I have resources you can't begin to imagine."

"When are you going to give me my sister's ledgers?"

"I'll have them delivered to Dan Hanks' hotel room in an hour. Check out what I say. You'll realize people are ready to rise up against Marcos. Then come back and see me."

Leigh limped out of the clinic, caught a cab. Maybe Rosa's ledgers wouldn't be of any use, even if Morales turned them over to her. He implied he knew something vital about her son. Would whatever it was help in her search?

Chapter XXVIII

Dan wasn't home when Leigh arrived at his hotel suite. She sat down to rest, deciding not to remove her disguise in case she had to go out again. A knock on the door startled her. She answered it. A messenger handed Leigh a heavy envelope. She tore off the top, dumped four blue folders on the table.

"Well, I'll be damned. Miguel delivered Rosa's ledgers."

She checked the first and last pages, lined them up by date, starting with 1955 through 1959. One was missing, 1960 through 1964. Miguel was holding out again. The missing ledger probably had information about her son. She scanned through the first ledger. Just as she had thought. Rosa's household budget, including records of sugar cane production. Losses were underlined in red pencil, along with notes to check business expenses with her husband, Raul.

Leigh went through another ledger, beginning January 1965. It was full of names, dates and sordid activities of people in San Carlos and the surrounding community. As Morales had said, it was a steamy diary. What had Rosa gotten into? And why? The remaining ledgers also contained gossip. Why had Miguel held onto one of them?

She must return to the seminary to get the missing folder from that bastard. No, his friends had probably moved him to a safer place. She would find out from Virgil later. Now she must go into the streets to hear what people thought about Ninoy's assassination. Her face flushed with anger. Morales had found another way to force her to do his bidding.

Leigh caught a cab to Rizal Park. People had tuned portable radios to news of Ninoy's assassination. They switched frequencies between government stations and Radio Veritas—the once unpopular station sponsored by the Catholic Church—to check the truth of official spokesmen. Leigh plopped down on a bench near a gathering crowd.

"Shot him in the back of the head," one woman said.

"Such cowardice," added another.

"They're blaming the Communists," a man said. "I don't believe them."

"Are we going to let them get away with it?" A young activist with long shaggy hair jumped up on a bench near Leigh.

A military sedan and several Jeeps screeched to a stop. Soldiers jumped out, stood at attention. An officer stepped out of the staff car.

"Get that man," he ordered, pointing toward Leigh—or the young orator. She wasn't certain.

Leigh gasped. It was General Fidel Navarro. She clutched her chest, struggling to breathe. She couldn't run with a sprained ankle. And there were too many soldiers to shoot her way out. Still, she reached for her gun.

Had they really seen through her disguise? No way. Displaying a weapon now wasn't the answer. She must continue the charade. But she had to get out of the way without attracting attention. Moving slowly—acting as if she wasn't a wanted criminal—Leigh sidled toward a masonry wall. Despite her effort to appear unconcerned, she hurried, stepping in a hole, twisting her injured ankle.

Leigh fell, dropping her bag, dark glasses slipping off. The glaring sun brought tears to her eyes. She shielded them, retrieved the sun glasses. Soldiers dashed to the activist, grabbed him. He struggled. One of them hit him with the butt of a rifle. As Leigh got to her feet, guilt washed over her. The young man was an innocent victim in the government search for Miguel. General Navarro strode up to her, arms folded across his chest.

"Are you all right, Old Man?"

Surprised by his thoughtfulness, Leigh nodded, avoiding his gaze, fearing he would recognize her.

"General, the boy did nothing wrong," a taxi driver said, expressing Leigh's thoughts.

"He's wanted for questioning in the death of a security guard at the airport," the General snapped.

"George has been studying here in Rizal Park since early morning," the cabbie replied.

People, initially frightened by the soldiers, moved forward to block their path. Had concern for the victim swept aside their fear? Some grumbled, becoming bolder as others crowded around. Soldiers fidgeted, apprehension replacing hostility.

"That's right," a vendor said, wiping his hands on a soiled apron. "He's been here since I opened up."

"Get out of the way," General Navarro snarled.

He, too, appeared uneasy. Tension continued to mount. More angry words were exchanged. Leigh cursed under her breath. This could end up in the death of innocent people. She must do something before the General ordered his men to shoot into the crowd.

Chapter XXIX

Hostilities between soldiers and civilians were about to explode. Leigh bit her lip, struggling to come up with a way to relieve the situation. An idea came to her.

"General, we'll sign statements that George was here in Rizal Park when the shooting took place," Leigh said. "That means he couldn't be the suspect you're looking for. Where are you taking him?"

"Fort Bonifacio," the General replied, tension fading from his face. "He'll be held over night. If you can prove he wasn't near the airport at the time the security guard was killed, I'll release him."

Grumbling, the crowd moved back. Soldiers dragged the young man to their vehicles. They tossed him in, drove away. Leigh sighed. General Navarro hadn't recognized her. And—though a fight had been avoided—he probably wouldn't release the young radical no matter how many witnesses came forward. Besides, those who could give George an alibi would likely back out. She walked slowly through the park, listening to people talk.

"General Ver killed him, but he's blaming Communists," a teen-age boy said. A middle-aged man hustled him into a car and drove away.

Some nodded agreement, but said nothing. Others cursed Marcos' Army Chief of Staff, then glanced furtively around as if fearing they would be overheard. A small group spoke out with reckless abandon. They gathered beneath the statue of Jose Rizal, the nineteenth century patriot for whom the park was dedicated. As she hurried to join them, Leigh twisted her ankle. Hobbling to the street, she caught a cab to Dan's hotel.

A note on the refrigerator read:

"Leigh, someone altered my message to Morales about Aquino's arrival on China Airlines. I gave a note to Fred Skarlotta. He had Cathy Valentine take it to Morales' man at Clark Air Base. I must look into this. See you after the funeral. Dan"

Leigh sighed in relief. She knew it. Dan had nothing to do with Ninoy's death. Were Skarlotta and Cathy involved? She shook her head. Had to be one of Morales' people. His group was riddled with spies.

Leigh got an ice-pack for her throbbing ankle, then sat down to think about what she had seen and heard. The people had shown unusual courage, voicing criticism of Marcos, even standing up to his soldiers. Would fear force them to abandon their new-found backbone? She tuned in Radio Veritas. The Catholic Church sponsored station's newscaster pointed an accusing finger of responsibility for Ninoy's death directly at the Philippine Army hierarchy.

"Ninoy Aquino's body has been recovered from the Army General Hospital by his mother who took it to his home where it will lie in state until his widow, Corazon, returns to the Philippines."

Leigh listened to the news, mulling over the issues as she cat-napped throughout the night. Early the next morning, she left the hotel, still in disguise.

"Take me to Times Street," she said to the taxi driver.

"Ninoy's house? I was going there myself, Grandfather."

They drove to the Aquino home, finding a parking place when another cab pulled away.

"It'll take me about fifteen minutes," the taxi driver said. "You coming?"

"Not now."

Leigh reached in her pocket and pulled out enough pesos to pay the fare. She got out and leaned against the vehicle, watching people enter. They came out with ashen faces. Max drove up. Leigh lifted her cane in greeting.

"Sit down and rest in my cab, Grandfather," Max said. "I'll be out in a few minutes."

Leigh got in his taxi. Max hadn't recognized her. Maybe she should have gone in too. She shook her head. Not yet.

"Rizal Park, Max," Leigh said when he returned.

"Leigh! Didn't know it was you. Good disguise."

When they arrived at the Park, Leigh set out in search of the taxi driver who spoke up to General Navarro. Unable to find him, she went to a push cart snack vendor.

"Did you go to Fort Bonifacio this morning?" Leigh asked.

"Sure did, Grandfather. Cabbie took us there to give sworn statements, but the guards wouldn't let us in."

"That's what I figured," Leigh said, limping away.

"If I knew where to go, I'd join the guerrillas," a young man sitting on the grass said.

"Me, too," his companion agreed.

They were determined to do something. Did people paying their respects to Ninoy feel the same way? She must return to the Aquino home. Max drove her back to Times Street.

"Park anywhere, Max. Taxi drivers, fish mongers and laborers came this morning. Looks like the rest of Manila is here now. Business men, office workers, well-dressed men and women—even the poor."

"Everyone looks like they seen a ghost when they come out. That's 'cause Ninoy looks the way he did right after they shot him, bloody clothes and all."

"Come on, Max, I've got to talk to Miguel."

Morales was listening to the radio when they entered a house near St. Andrew's Hospital.

"Ninoy's body will be taken to his hometown of Concepcion where people of Tarlac Province, unable to come to Manila, can pay their respects," the news reporter said.

Morales turned off the radio. "I knew you'd come to see me about the missing diary."

"I should have known you'd hold out on me."

"Oh, I don't have it. Never did. I just didn't tell you it was missing."

"Then who does?" Leigh asked.

"Sumo's cousins, Rufo and Vic Sobel. They decided to go into the blackmail business for themselves."

"Where are they?"

"The police picked them up on a burglary charge. They're serving time in a labor camp somewhere. Don't know where at the moment, but I can find out."

"And you'll tell me?"

"Yes, but you'll have to use your own guerrillas to get the diary back."

What guerrillas? She didn't have any guerrillas and Morales knew it. She didn't even know how to recruit them. Damn. He had her over a barrel again.

Several days later, Corazon Aquino announced plans for the funeral. This would be Leigh's last chance to view his body. She got up at four the next morning, wrapped her ankle, then put on heavy stockings and comfortable shoes, slipped into a black dress. She applied a dab of makeup and lipstick, donned sunglasses. Tying a yellow scarf around her head to honor Ninoy Aquino, she left. Max was asleep in his cab.

"I knew you'd come out early, Leigh," he said, rubbing his eyes. "Going without disguise?"

"I'll be lost in the crowd—I hope."

Hours before the funeral Mass was scheduled to begin mourners started to congregate. Three plump middle-aged women clutched rosary beads as they entered the church. Leigh shuffled down the aisle behind them. When they stopped at a pew, she moved forward to Ninoy's open casket. Dried blood covered his face, except where it had chipped off preparing his death mask. She knelt and crossed herself. Could she commit herself to a revolution as Miguel had asked? Not if it would hinder the search for her son. Maybe she could do both.

Leigh got up, found a seat at the end of a pew next to the plump middle-aged women. The nave was soon overflowing. Many worshipers stood in the aisles. Stifling air reeked of sweating bodies, colognes and perfumes. Hand-held fans worked vigorously.

When Mass ended, pall-bearers carried Senator Aquino's casket out, placed it on a flat-bed truck. Leigh shuffled along with hundreds of thousands as the funeral cortege crawled toward a cemetery thirty kilometers away. Unseasonal showers brought a welcome relief. Clothes soaked, ankle aching and stomach growling, Leigh inched forward until the procession finally reached its destination.

Night had fallen before she found a taxi for the return trip. She settled back against the seat, groaning, closing her eyes. She awoke when the cab pulled up to Dan's hotel.

"Better get out of those wet clothes," Dan said when she entered his suite.

Leigh dropped into a chair. "I got up at four this morning to go to Ninoy's funeral. I'm just getting back. Do you know what that means?"

"More than a million people turned out. It was bigger than Gandhi's funeral. The world will have to take notice, and Marcos must act accordingly."

"Act accordingly?" Leigh asked.

"He can't white-wash Aquino's death. He has to appoint a commission to bring those responsible up on charges."

"We can't sit back and let it go at that."

"That's all you can do now."

"People will rise up against him, Dan. Miguel wants me to organize a guerrilla force and become a part of it."

"You can't do that."

"I have no other choice."

"Then you're on your own."

Dan didn't understand. And she was too tired to explain. A quarrel would only bring anger, and she didn't want cherished memories tarnished. Leigh clutched her breast. Oh Lord, this was the end of their relationship, and it was worse than she had imagined.

Dan glowered. Running a hand through his hair, he shook his head. Would he say something to start an argument? That was the last thing she wanted. She sniffed back tears.

"Don't cry," Dan said, kissing her. "I don't understand why you're doing what you are, but I know how you feel."

"Then why did you say, I'll be on my own?"

"I can't get helicopter support from our people in the Philippine Air Force."

"I thought you were dumping me, Dan. Should have known I could count on you."

"You're not giving up the search for your son?"

"Of course not. Morales says he knows where to find him. He may be lying, but I can't take any chances. So I'm going to train a band of guerrillas to get Rosa's ledger."

"I thought he was going to give them to you."

"He gave me what he had, but the important ledger is missing, the one that includes the time my son was born."

"Why do you need guerrillas to help you get it?" Dan asked.

"Miguel says Sumo's cousins have the ledger, and they're confined in a labor camp. As soon as he finds out where, I have to break them out."

"Are you sure what you need is in that ledger? How about duplicate hospital records?"

"I must get hold of Marci and ask her to search her house in San Carlos for medical records her father took home from the hospital," Leigh replied. "She's been avoiding me."

Dan looked at his watch. "I'm sorry, Leigh. I'd like to stay and talk, but I've got to go out."

"Where are you going?"

"Malacanang Palace. Marcos is giving a reception for American Senator Hatfield."

"They're having a party on the night of Aquino's funeral? Dan, you can't go."

"I'm a spy—your spy. If I don't go and be nice to those bastards, I'll blow my cover. Then I'd be useless to you, when—or if—your rebellion ever develops."

"Okay, I'll forgive you since it's for a good cause. But don't stay any longer than necessary to pacify those State Department slime balls."

After Dan left, Leigh flexed her arms, grimacing. Every muscle in her body cried out for relief. She turned on the faucet, removed her clothes and stepped into the tub. The water was hot—almost too hot—but it soothed her aches and pains. When finished, she dried herself, trudged to the bed and crawled in.

Sleep refused to come, her mind in turmoil. Would Miguel locate Sumo's cousins? Could she find Marci, then pressure the young woman into turning over her late father's duplicate hospital records?

Leigh was still awake when Dan tip-toed into the bedroom. He undressed and slipped between the sheets. Passion rekindled, forcing problems from her mind. Her breath quickening, she put her arms around his neck, pulled him against her warm beckoning body.

Chapter XXX

Paulita and Max recruited guerrillas, then helped Leigh train them. Miguel, however, hadn't found Sumo's cousins, Rufo and Vic Sobel. His excuses angered Leigh. Still, she could do nothing about it. Marci continued to avoid her. Leigh went to Virgil for help.

"Go on the demonstration against Marcos today and you'll find Marci," he said.

"If there's no other way to pin her down, I'll join her damn Communist protest march."

"They're only college kids on a peaceful demonstration. Communists might exploit the situation, but they would hardly settle for such a mild protest. Besides, your group wants to get rid of Marcos by revolution too."

"That may be true, but I'm going to turn my guerrillas over to Max as soon as I get the information I need from the Sobels, if Morales ever finds them. Anyway, you felt the same way once."

"That was when I had legs, Auntie Leigh."

Leigh heard the despair in Virgil's voice. Oh Lord, how could she have been so insensitive? She dropped to her knees, took him in her arms.

"I love you just as you are, Virgil. I don't know what I'd do without you."

"I'm all right most of the time. I do get depressed when I think about how the doctors can't remove the bullet from my back. You'd better go if you're going to find Marci."

"I can't leave you the way you're feeling."

"I'm okay now."

Leigh, dressed in shirt and baggy trousers, no make-up, horned-rimmed glasses and upper body wrapped to hide her breasts, had Max drive her to the demonstration.

"They're already marching," she said as Max drove up behind a throng of protesters. "Drop me at the corner."

"I'll pick up Miguel and take him to the bus station, then come back for you, Leigh. We got to return to camp tomorrow. Paulita can't get around on that bad leg."

Leigh hurried through marchers, cursing Communists—red bands around their heads—carrying red banners. Why had college kids with yellow T-shirts and head bands honoring Ninoy Aquino joined them? The demonstrators blocked her path. Leigh was about to abandon her search, then realized everyone had stopped.

"Got to move barricades out of the way so we can get to Malacanang Palace," a demonstrator said.

My God, they were going to march right up to President Marcos' doorstep. Maybe Marci was at the head of the parade. Shoving protesters aside, Leigh reached the front of the demonstration. The dumb kids were throwing rocks at police. She spotted Marci moving a barricade. Water gushing from high-pressure hoses knocked the young woman off her feet. As Leigh ran to Marci, a stream of water washed both of them into the gutter.

"Quick, into that doorway," Leigh said, dragging Marci to a building.

A fusillade of shots erupted, bringing screams of fear. The marchers scattered, bullets ricocheting off street and sidewalk by their feet.

"Police are ambushing the demonstrators," Leigh shouted.

"They're shooting my friends. I've got to do something."

"Damn it, Marci, stay put!"

A hail of police bullets cut down protesters. Friends went to their aid. They, too, were felled. Those who tried to get away were also hit. Shrieks of pain knifed through the barrage of automatic weapons fire. Blood, spurting from the wounded, splattered on companions, onto the street and sidewalks. A few injured demonstrators struggled to their feet, then escaped with the help of friends. Nearly two dozen, however, lay dead.

"We've got to do something," Marci yelled, dashing into the cross-fire.

Leigh started after her, then backed away as bullets whined off the sidewalk in front of her. She wasn't going to risk her life in a Communist demonstration despite concern for the young woman. Bravery was exactly what Leigh wanted in guerrillas, and Marci had plenty of that. But she was going to get killed.

"Marci, get back here. I need you."

Marci bent over a boy covered with blood, shook her head and hurried to another, and another. Finally, she tried to drag an unconscious young man toward the doorway, bullets whining around her. Though nearly as tall, Marci lacked Leigh's strength. Leigh ran to Marci's aid, helped her carry the wounded boy to the building, then put a bandage over a gaping wound in his upper thigh.

White smoke billowed from canisters thrown by the police. Tear gas. Eyes stinging, Leigh wrapped more bandages around the young man's thigh, binding them tightly. They quickly turned red. His pulse weakened, then stopped.

"This boy's dead," she said.

"I've got to help my friends." Rubbing her burning eyes, Marci rose.

"It was dumb luck you didn't get your head blown off, Marci. And that's what'll happen if you go out there again. Police will put on gas masks and pick us up. We've got to get out of here."

Marci pulled out of Leigh's grasp, ran into the street to help a wounded girl crawling toward them. Leigh sighed when she got back safely.

"She's dead too, Marci. Come on, let's move."

Yielding to Leigh's demand, Marci tried the handle on the door behind her. Locked. She wrapped a bandana around her fist, smashed a pane of glass, then reached in, opened it and entered. Leigh picked up her knapsack and followed. She shuffled along an unlighted corridor behind Marci. Pulling a sheathed bayonet out of her back-pack, Leigh fastened it under her pants leg. She grabbed a flashlight, slung the pack over her shoulder, pistol still inside.

Reaching the rear exit, Leigh and Marci went into the alleyway. As they neared a side street, demonstrators ran toward them, a police car in pursuit. Another government vehicle drove in from the opposite end. They were trapped.

Chapter XXXI

Police herded Leigh and Marci into a van along with four student demonstrators. A broad-shouldered officer got in behind them. Another closed and locked the door from the outside. Leigh figured someone would recognize her at police headquarters. She must escape before they got there. Dan couldn't help. He was out of the country.

Pistol drawn, the guard moved in front of Leigh, spun the chamber, placed the barrel against her forehead. The son-of-a-bitch was trying to scare her. Beaded sweat rolled down her brow into her eyes when he squeezed the trigger. It clicked. She sighed. The gun had misfired. Or had it?

The officer laughed maniacally. "I forgot to load that chamber with one of my hollow-point bullets. You're lucky. It would've taken your head off."

He sidled to the next captive, spun the chamber, put the barrel against a demonstrator's head and squeezed the trigger. Another click. Had the gun misfired again? No, the hammer had fallen on an empty chamber. She could see bullets in the other chambers. My God, the bastard was playing Russian roulette! As he stepped in front of the next victim, Leigh knew she must do something or someone would be killed.

Hey, they forgot to search her. She still had her pistol and bayonet. How could she divert the guard's attention? Leigh nudged Marci.

"Flirt with him."

"No talking," the officer growled, pointing his gun at Leigh. "Let me have that back-pack."

"I'm a d-d-doctor," Leigh stammered, standing up, taking off her back-pack. "I was on my way to catch a bus when the riot broke out. I was treating innocent bystanders when you picked me up with these Communist terrorists."

Leigh moved toward the officer, handing him her back-pack. As he reached out, Leigh shoved it against his gun arm. Kicking him on the knee cap, she snatched the bayonet from her boot and plunged it into his stomach. Disbelief washed over his face, eyes glazed, blood spewing from his mouth. The officer's gun fired as she wrenched it from his hand. He slumped to the floor. The van stopped abruptly, throwing Leigh forward, striking her head. She staggered to the door, shot the lock off, expecting the officers in the front to come at her with guns blazing.

"You're on your own," Leigh said to the demonstrators.

Grabbing Marci's hand, she jumped down, glancing around, praying Max had returned.

"Over here, Leigh," Max yelled.

The police started shooting, but took cover when Max opened up with an automatic weapon.

Leigh and Marci scrambled into his cab. Max sped away, tires squealing. Taking the corner on two wheels, he slammed into a car, glanced off. Flooring the accelerator, he turned at the next intersection and broke into traffic.

"I saw them pick you up and followed," Max said.

Leigh rubbed the lump on her head, looked at Marci's ashen face. "Virgil told me you were going to join the guerrillas. Why did you change your mind?"

"My uncles pressured me to stay away from them."

"They want you to get involved with Communists?" Leigh asked.

"They don't like that either."

"Marci, are you, or are you not going to join us?"

"I don't want to go against my family, but..."

"I need to talk to you before you get killed with your damn foolishness. Tell me about the duplicate hospital records your parents took home."

"I'm sorry, Leigh. A fire destroyed all but a few of them. You can have what remains."

"Oh God. Okay, get them as soon as you can. Well, are you with us or not?"

"I can't just do nothing after what happened today."

"Pack your bag. We leave for camp in the morning."

Even as Leigh finished training her guerrillas, she found time to study the medical records Marci had given her. Several partially burned documents attracted her attention. She could make out the name of Antonio Navarro on a birth certificate and adoption papers. Leigh had used Navarro, Rosa's married name, when she checked into Dr. Zurate's hospital for the birth of her child. Oh my God, that was Sumo's legal name. That overgrown ape couldn't have been her son, could he? She must find someone who could bring out information on the scorched documents. And she had to get Rosa's missing ledger. It would provide answers.

Leigh went to Morales' nipa-hut. "Miguel, have you found Sumo's cousins?"

"I'm working on it," he replied.

"If you don't come up with something soon, you can take this job and shove it."

"Stay with me, Leigh. I'll have something soon."

Leigh went back to work. She was pleased so many young men and women took readily to the training, especially Marci. A few couldn't keep up, and Paulita was no longer physically able to perform as an instructor. Leigh had to find something else for her to do—something important. She ordered the misfits and Paulita to come to her nipa-hut.

"We've got problems," Leigh said.

"You can't hack the program," Paulita interrupted. "It isn't from lack of trying. But the bottom line is, you'll get your friends killed if you become guerrillas. And so will I, with this game leg."

"You're right, Paulita, but I have a job for you that's too important to trust to just anyone. What was the one thing you needed most when you prepared for an operation?"

"Weapons, ammunition and good intelligence," Paulita replied.

"You're all from Metro-Manila. What's the Board of Inquiry that Marcos was forced to appoint doing about Ninoy Aquino's murder?"

"Two days ago, the Agrava Board accused General Ver," Paulita replied. "Marcos has relieved him as Chief of Staff, but kept him on as military advisor."

"Yeah, but we receive only information they want us to have. We don't know what's going on inside the government."

"What difference does it make?" Paulita asked.

"It'll be vitally important when we're ready to strike in Marcos' back yard."

"You're going to move our whole company to Metro-Manila, all 120 guerrillas?"

"As soon as we get equipment. Paulita, can you organize a network of agents to infiltrate the military and gather the intelligence information we'll need to launch a full scale attack against Marcos?"

"One company of guerrillas is like a drop in the bucket. Several companies—or even battalions—couldn't take on the whole Philippine Army."

"That's the idea behind your group. Your job is to find out who will defect, who will join us and who will remain neutral. We need to know exactly how many will be with us and how many against us."

"You'll get your intelligence network," Paulita said, putting out her hand.

Leigh took it, looking askance at the others. They joined hands.

"First, see if you can find Sumo's cousins, Rufo and Vic Sobel. Miguel says they're in a labor camp, but he can't locate it. And look for my nephew's friend, Carl. He's disappeared from St. Andrew's Seminary, and Virgil's getting worried."

Chapter XXXII

Paulita couldn't locate Virgil's friend, Carl. She had, however, no trouble finding the Sobels in a labor camp near Lingayen. Leigh was pleased to get the news, but angry that Morales couldn't find them. She sent a team to Lingayen to gather information. On returning, the intelligence officer reported the camp defended by minimum security forces. A squad of guerrillas could overrun them. At last, Leigh would get Rosa's missing ledger. She prepared an operations plan to attack the facility and free Sumo's cousins. She showed it to Morales for approval.

"Nothing wrong with your plan, but you've made a serious mistake," Miguel said.

"What's that?"

"This is based on information that may not be valid when you're ready to attack."

Damn, she should have left an intelligence officer there to keep an eye out for changes.

"Okay, I'll hold up until we check it out."

Leigh sent Max to Lingayen. When he returned, she knew something was wrong by the expression on his face.

"They've moved the prisoners to a new labor camp on my family farm at San Carlos," Max said.

"Go get the information we need, then leave a man there to monitor the situation."

When Max returned with intelligence data, Leigh prepared an operations plan and took it to Morales.

"You're sure the camp will still be in business when you're ready?" he asked.

"We left a cadre at San Carlos to keep an eye on things. How come you couldn't find the Sobels? Paulita had no trouble."

"I did find them, then fed the information to Paulita because I didn't think you'd believe me. Anyway, I can't give you any help on this operation."

"We can handle it."

The next morning, Leigh led Max's platoon of thirty-six guerrillas on its first major operation. Marci commanded another platoon that was poorly equipped, and armed with World War II Garand rifles. Her platoon wouldn't be effective, except to back-up the main attack.

"Damn it, Leigh, I joined up to fight, and you put us in reserve," Marci cried.

"You don't have the fire-power."

"Yeah, I know. Okay, we'll set up an ambush to cover your retreat."

As her guerrillas neared the Garcia farm, doubts flooded into Leigh's mind. She shook it off. Rosa's ledger and the Japanese gold were there. This operation had to succeed.

"Max, spread your troops out and move through the forest. Scouts on the flanks. You take the center. Radio silence until you reach the observation point."

Max called a few minutes later. "At the O.P. and holding, Nightingale."

Leigh clicked her transmitter, crept forward to join him.

"What do we have, Max?"

"General Navarro's troops found the gold and how to get around the booby trap. See the lights on the hill back of the barn, and the people milling around?"

"I see civilian workers loading a truck."

"The infantry company will be down to platoon strength, Leigh, with those three vehicles pulling away now. That'll leave one truck and two personnel carriers."

Leigh raised infrared binoculars, panning the farm, settling on the lighted area Max had mentioned.

"Not having to take on an infantry company is a break, but I don't like losing so much gold."

"I can cut cross-country with a squad and ambush the vehicles that just left," Max said. "With the gold they're carrying, and what remains here, we'll make out."

"Okay, but if you hear us in a fire fight before you're in position, hustle back."

"Why start a fight before I've had a chance to set up the ambush?"

"I don't want to, but I'm not going to let the soldiers kill the civilian workers."

Leigh set up machine guns for a cross fire, then ordered her guerrillas to move through waist-high grass, slapping at bugs buzzing around her head. Finally reaching a clearing, she snaked along the ground to rusty farm equipment.

Eight enemy guards were climbing into the back of a truck filled with gold bars. The vehicle moved forward, soldiers manning machine guns on personnel carriers.

"Ready," Leigh radioed, now certain they were going to kill the workers.

The truck stopped. Enemy troops alongside personnel carriers raised their rifles, aiming at the civilian workers. Machine gunners charged rounds into chambers.

"Fire," Leigh ordered.

Guerrillas opened up, bullets whistling across the peaceful countryside, cutting down machine gunners. Tracers streaked through the night, some ricocheting off metal objects, whining into the black sky. Most smashed into soldiers. The battle ended a few minutes after it started, the enemy raising their hands in surrender. Ordering a cease fire, Leigh moved forward. Blood was splattered everywhere.

Twenty soldiers dead, sixteen wounded. Guerrillas gathered their weapons.

Squad leaders rounded up civilian workers. As Leigh checked the gold, she heard a laboring automobile engine approaching. She stared into darkness trying to locate the vehicle. Headlights flashed into her eyes.

"What shall we do?" a squad leader radioed.

"Stand by."

As soon as the vehicle moved a little closer, she would attack. The truck inched forward. Leigh pressed the radio transmitter button to give the order to open fire.

"Leigh, is that you?" a voice yelled.

"Hold your fire, it's Max," Leigh radioed. "Turn off the headlights, Max," she continued. "And get out where we can see you."

Max and his men jumped to the ground.

"Why didn't you call us?" Leigh asked.

"Our radio was shot up. We spotted a squad of soldiers around this truck watching the driver change a flat tire."

"Why did you take them on?"

"Couldn't get by to set up the ambush. Anyway, when I heard your fire fight, we killed the soldiers, fixed the tire and came back with this truck full of gold."

"The army will return to investigate the shooting. Pass out the gold and let's move out."

"We have to use some of the civilians," Max said.

"Take as many as you need, then send the others into San Carlos with the wounded soldiers. Make sure the Sobels are with us."

Leigh led the guerrillas and fifty civilians into the mountains, loaded with weapons, ammunition and gold. An hour later, Marci's platoon welcomed them. Sight of the gold brought a premature celebration.

"Back off," Leigh ordered. "Get the civilians seated so I can count heads."

Four, including the Sobels, were missing, along with gold bars they had carried.

"Marci, take a squad and find them. Bring the Sobels back alive."

Leigh ordered the others to rest until dawn. At sun-up, she led the balance of two platoons and the civilian workers to her permanent camp site.

That evening, Marci returned empty handed. "The two civilians who escaped are dead, Leigh. The Sobels must have killed them for the gold, then headed down river."

"That's what we should have done."

"If other guerrilla leaders learn about our gold we'll have a fight on our hands," Marci said.

"They've probably already heard," Max replied. "We better haul it down river in fishing boats."

"Okay, Max, use your platoon," Leigh said. "At Lingayen put the gold aboard our medical supply boat and head for Hong Kong. Take a squad with you and send the others back here. I'll fly to Hong Kong and make arrangements to buy weapons."

"That's where the Sobels are headed," Marci said. "I know them, Leigh. I should go with you."

"Okay, you and I'll fly to Hong Kong. The civilians we released will talk, Max, so expect trouble all the way."

"When do we leave?"

"Right now."

"It's dangerous on the river at night."

"And it's too risky to wait until morning."

Chapter XXXIII

In Hong Kong, Marci searched for the Sobels while Leigh exchanged gold for U.S. dollars. She bought weapons and ammunition from a dealer Miguel lined up. Max loaded everything aboard his boat and sailed for the Philippines.

Marci drove up in a taxi as Leigh watched Max leave. Leigh raised her eyebrows. "What did you learn?"

"My leads were good," Marci replied. "I located the Sobels in a hotel, then staked it out. I spotted them this morning with Virgil's friend, Carl."

"What's he doing with them?"

"Miguel says he does contract work for their family."

"Assassination?"

"Among other things," Marci replied.

"Why did he latch onto my nephew?"

"Probably thought Virgil knew something about gold buried on the Garcia farm. When that didn't work out, he split. Anyway, I followed the Sobels to bankers who deal in stolen gold."

"They still have our gold?"

"I'm sure of it. One of the places they visited was the banker who gave us the highest bid. Miguel was there, doing business with one of the partners, but they didn't see him."

"Where's Miguel now?" Leigh asked.

"He's waiting for them to return with the gold. Want to go back and pick them up?"

"I've got to check out their hotel room first," Leigh replied. "Give me the key. You did get a key, didn't you?"

"Yeah, I bribed the desk clerk. Room 406. Want me to go with you?"

"Stay with Miguel, Marci. I'll tear the room apart and find Rosa's ledger, then join you."

Later, Leigh drove up in a cab at the gold banker's place of business. Marci jumped in.

"Let's get out of here," Marci said in Tagalog.

Leigh gave the driver instructions in English, then turned back to Marci. "What happened?"

"We got in a fire fight with the Sobels and killed them. Did you find what you were looking for?"

"Not a thing. Did you search the brothers?"

"The gold was all they had on them. Miguel turned it over to the banker and pocketed the money. Carl must have your sister's diary, Leigh. He was with the Sobels until they went to the banker."

"He's probably on his way back to the Philippines now that the gold isn't available. Let's go home, Marci."

As soon as they arrived at her base camp, Leigh put out feelers for Carl, then started training new guerrillas. On returning from Hong Kong the following week, Morales called her to his nipa-hut.

"I got the diary you've been looking for," he said, handing her a soiled blue ledger.

Leigh stammered her thanks, returned to her hut. She shook her head. This was so unlike Miguel. She shrugged. Maybe he was making up for pocketing the money he got for the gold the Sobels had stolen from her.

Leigh scanned Rosa's ledger, stopping to read comments about Raul's drinking and mismanagement of their sugar cane business. She frowned at an entry dated April 26, 1961, then snapped her fingers.

"Rosa's 37th birthday."

Leigh read on:

"October 2, 1961. Raul mortgaged the farm, then spent every penny on whiskey for his friends at the Songbird and on a 'cure' for impotency by some quack doctor. The bank is going to foreclose on my house if I don't do something soon. Raul says he can get the money from his half-brother, but I must agree to an experimental medical program that frightens me, or to an alternate proposal so immoral it's disgusting."

Leigh turned the page. Figures showing what Rosa and Raul owed, and too little money to pay. Other entries were filled with her sister's depressive thoughts, and of going to church to pray for guidance. Ten pages later, Leigh found another informative entry.

"October 12, 1961. I finally agreed to Raul's disgusting proposal of going to bed with his half-brother, Fidel. It makes me sick, but I'm afraid to try the experimental medical procedure. Raul says his doctor worked with a research group in England that had great success. If we don't have a child soon, Raul's crazy father will donate all his money and properties to some heathen church. Fidel inherits one-fourth the estate if Raul and I have a baby, nothing otherwise."

Leigh looked up and frowned. Had Raul's doctor been involved with experiments in artificial insemination that were years ahead of the first test tube baby? Maybe, maybe not. Hey, it didn't make any difference. Raul had been diagnosed as impotent, not infertile.

Leigh continued reading. There were more entries of Rosa worrying about losing her home, and fear of being too old to have children. On October 31, 1961, she wrote:

"Fidel tonight."

A note the following day:

"November 1, 1961. Went to the Songbird Tavern with Raul and Fidel. I drank two glasses of wine for courage. Still, I couldn't go through with it. I was so ashamed of even considering it, I ordered Fidel out of the house. When I had calmed down, I asked Raul about his doctor's medical procedure. He assured me—if it worked—he would be the real father of our baby. We'll see his doctor tonight."

"General Fidel Navarro came close to being Virgil's father," Leigh said aloud. "And it could have happened the same night that bastard raped me."

Leigh's face flushed with anger. She continued reading of her sister's guilt and shame. Entries two months later mentioned Rosa's pregnancy—but not how—and the happiness it brought; Raul getting money from Fidel to pay the bank; his father sending an allowance for the expected child; and of Rosa's fury when she learned Leigh was also pregnant.

"January 2, 1962. People are going to talk, and I've got to protect myself. I know about the skeletons in their closets. That won't keep them from gossiping about me unless I record everything, then threaten to expose them if they don't keep their mouths shut."

"That's why Rosa turned her ledgers into diaries," Leigh mumbled. "She was blackmailing her neighbors."

The rest of the pages, until the final one dated July 25, 1962, were filled with gossip. Rosa mentioned her intent to join Leigh at Dr. Zurate's hospital in the hills.

"Let's see, I went there in February when I started to show," Leigh mumbled. "Hey, there should be more pages."

She looked at the binding. Someone had cut everything out after July. Miguel? Possibly. What about Marci? She wouldn't have any reason. Besides, she didn't even have the ledger. Carl might be the one. Oh Lord, it would be as hard to find him as it was to pin down Miguel. What a bummer. Leigh was no closer to finding her son than when she came to the Philippines. If only Paulita could locate Carl. And if she could just find a way to force Miguel to give her a straight answer.

Leigh agonized over one failure after another. Carl had vanished. Leigh put pressure on Miguel, even threatened to quit to force him to tell her everything he knew. He eventually opened up, but Leigh was certain he was holding something back.

Then Dan Hanks located a government official who agreed to provide duplicate documents of people born in Pangasinan Province about the same time as Virgil.

"I've found our man, Leigh," Dan said. "He wanted $25,000, but I got him down to $15,000."

"I have $6,500, Dan. I'll find a way to get the rest."

"He wants half now and the balance on delivery. I can come up with a thousand now, and I can get another $3,000 by the end of next month. It'll take my man that long to smuggle the documents out of the building."

"I can go to Miguel for the balance, but he'll want me to stay with him till the end of the year."

Chapter XXXIV

Max drove a dirty red and white bus heading for Manila with a special group of guerrillas. Aboard, Leigh, dressed in worn work clothes, horned rimmed glasses and sombrero, had glued a mustache to her upper lip. Twenty-three male and twenty-four female guerrillas, disguised as provincials on a shopping spree, were with her. This was the last of many trips smuggling weapons, ammunition and explosives into the metropolitan area for Morales' planned attack on Marcos' Army.

"Leigh, there's a roadblock ahead," Max yelled.

"What's going on?"

"They're tearing all the trucks apart. We can't pull out of line without attracting attention."

"Okay, everyone follow my lead," Leigh said. "We'll bluff our way through this."

As Max stopped at the inspection station, Leigh took the hand of a women, escorted her down the steps. The other men and women got off as couples, heading for rest rooms. A policeman, about to board, stepped aside.

"Sorry, officer," Max said. "They been after me to stop, but we was running late. Who you looking for?"

"They all have to go to the 'john' at the same time? Pull out of line, then get the hell out of here when they come back."

When the "provincials" returned, Max drove away. Leigh sat back, closed her eyes. Lord, she was tired. Morales' plan to attack Marcos' armed forces was about to become a reality. She had been up all night preparing a briefing for guerrilla commanders. Leigh had accepted the task, believing she could force him to reveal all he knew about her child if she hit him at an opportune moment.

The bus entered Metro-Manila. Max turned off the thoroughfare, drove along a secondary road, then into a driveway beside an old house. Paulita opened the doors to a barn-like garage, closed them after he drove in. The guerrillas pulled up a false floor in the vehicle, removed weapons and ammunition as Paulita took Leigh to the house.

"When I learned of the roadblock, it was too late to warn you, Leigh. How did you get through?"

"Max's idea of making up the platoon with an equal number of men and women threw the inspectors off-guard. How long are the police going to continue the roadblocks?"

"I don't know, but we'll have to hold up our execution date until we know for sure. We can't get all of our troops into Manila now. This is the first trouble we've had, but it comes at a critical time."

"Have you told the commanders to stay put until we give the go-ahead?"

"Yeah, they'll wait for your return to camp."

"When do you think we can go after Marcos?" Leigh asked.

"Probably have to hold off a month or two. Better check it out with Miguel."

"Can we count on Reform the Armed Forces Movement?"

"They'll probably defect, but not to us," Paulita replied. "The military men who formed RAM are still loyal to the government. They want Marcos to provide better equipment and leadership. If he turns them down again, they'll revolt, but won't support Communists."

"They think I'm a Communist?"

"They think anyone opposed to Marcos is a Communist, except themselves, of course."

"I can understand how it happens. We need better public relations. Okay, we'll take what help we can get. You're sure our supporters in the military have convinced the officers in their units to join us?"

"Sure as I can be," Paulita replied. "That'll give us help from three battalions. What about guerrilla leaders?"

"Jun and Revie will be here. The others will go along, but only in the areas where they normally operate."

"They'll get on board if we're still in business a week after the attack starts."

"If they keep pressure on the army in their areas of operations, the government can't reinforce the units we'll be going up against. Anyway, the guerrilla leaders don't know about our friends in the Philippine Army. How about our reserve cadres, Paulita?"

"We have 2,400 civilians on alert. Max's special platoon deserves a pat on the back for getting weapons and ammo for them. Did you bring any heavy weapons?"

"Everything except anti-aircraft guns," Leigh replied. "I'll check your Operations Plan before I go back to camp. Miguel can give the execution order verbally to cut down leaks. Anything on Carl?"

"He's back in the Philippines," Paulita replied. "You still think he's got those missing pages from your sister's diary? What about Miguel?"

"I'm certain Carl has them. Miguel knows something, but he'll hold out to the bitter end. Somehow, I'll get it out of him. What about the burned documents from Marci?"

"Sorry, Leigh, but we could bring out only the father's name on Sumo's birth certificate, Fidel Navarro."

"I already know that. What I don't know is whether or not I'm Sumo's birth mother. It's driving me crazy."

"I can imagine. Anyway, we picked up Carl's trail when he went to the American Embassy last week. Don't know who he talked to. He gave us the slip, then we discovered he'd flown to Guam. Thought we'd lost him, but he's here now."

"Anything from Dan?" Leigh asked.

"He wants to see you before he goes to California. He got a list of people born the same time as Virgil from an assistant recorder in Pangasinan Province. You better clean up and change."

Paulita held up her manicured fingernails. Leigh frowned at her own calloused hands, then glanced in the mirror. She dashed to the bedroom, took off her clothes and got under a shower. When dressed, she put an automatic pistol in her purse and walked to the thoroughfare to hail a cab.

Dan opened the door as Leigh fumbled for her key. She took off sun glasses, set them on the table with her purse and went into his arms, kissing him passionately.

"Seems like forever since I've seen you, Dan. Paulita said your man in the recorder's office delivered."

"Not until he put the bite on me for $10,000 more."

"You gave him another $10,000? If I'd been able to get to Manila more often, I could have saved you some money."

"I don't think so, Leigh. The assistant recorder high-tailed it to the States because Morales threatened to kill him for releasing the list."

"Why?"

"That's a puzzler, unless Morales knows something and realized you'll learn what it is when you start checking. Here are the names. I think you should concentrate on four of them."

"Why just four?"

"Three boys and a girl were born to unwed mothers, and Dr. Zurate was the attending physician."

"That makes sense," Leigh said.

"I don't recognize the birth mothers of three, but a baby was still-born to Leighanne Navarro. That was you, wasn't it, Leigh?"

"Yes, but I don't think that's the way it happened. I need more information, Dan. Anything on Marci's story of her parents' duplicate medical records being burned?"

"I'll check that out after I get back from Oakland."

Dan kissed her again. Leigh felt her passion coming alive. She unbuttoned his shirt, slid her hands onto his bare flesh. Arms around each other, they hurried to the bedroom, slipping out of their clothes. Her breath quickened. She caressed scars crisscrossing his rippling chest and taut stomach muscles. Pulling aside covers, Leigh and Dan slid between sheets. Nights of loneliness faded from her mind. Overcome with desire, she gave him her unbridled love.

Later, they lay side by side, holding hands, snuggling together.

"I'm worried about you going to Oakland, Dan."

"No more than I worry about you. Is Morales ready to start his revolution?"

"Will be soon. Did you ever straighten out your problem with Ninoy's arrival?"

"Miguel was hard to convince. He had as much trouble believing Fred Skarlotta was behind it as I did. By the way, don't talk to Cathy about your plans."

"I haven't seen her in months. Where is she, and why shouldn't I talk to her?"

"She's on her way here from Guam with Fred. They should be landing any time. I was going to leave for California this morning, but Skarlotta got wind of what I was doing and called. I agreed to a meeting because I wanted to see you."

"Why is Cathy with Skarlotta? She can't be involved in this mess. She told me all about herself and her..."

"Her family?"

"Come to think of it, she avoided talking about them every time I tried to get her to open up."

"Cathy didn't tell you Fred Skarlotta was her uncle?"

"Her uncle? I can't believe it."

"I think Skarlotta killed my wife and son, but I won't be certain until I see my contact in Oakland."

"My God, he's supposed to be your friend. Why did you invite him here?"

"I keep hoping I'm wrong," Dan replied. "I had to give him this last chance to come up with an explanation."

A knock at the door. Dan jumped out of bed, put on a robe and headed for the sitting room.

"Fred may be early. Stay here, Leigh."

Leigh slipped into a robe, sat on the edge of the bed. Suddenly a feeling of danger washed over her. Oh Lord, Skarlotta could have sent an assassin to kill Dan. She jumped up, then realized her gun was in her purse on the table at the entry. She yanked open the drawer of the night stand, grabbed Dan's revolver. Racing to the sitting room, she heard a shot ring out, followed by a muffled thump. Was she too late?

Chapter XXXV

A bald-headed young man, face pale, eyes glazed, slumped back against the door. Blood covered the front of his shirt. His legs buckled. He collapsed, his gun—silencer attached—dropped on the floor beside him.

Dan turned to Leigh, automatic in one hand, the other clutching his side, blood seeping through his fingers. She ran to him.

"I'm okay, Leigh. Burns like hell, and I'm bleeding all over the place, but it's only a flesh wound."

"Lie down, I'll have a look."

Leigh helped Dan to the couch, opened his robe, nodded, then got a medical kit.

"It'll be sore for a few days, Dan, but I don't think the bullet hit any vital organs. I'll dress the wound and give you some antibiotics. You better see a doctor to be on the safe side. How did you get the gun? You left yours in the drawer by the bed."

"I grabbed the automatic pistol from your purse."

"Thank God, I left it on the stand by the door. Why did you let this assassin into the apartment?"

"Don't you recognize Carl? That's what threw me off. I didn't know he was on Skarlotta's payroll."

"I've been trying to find him."

"Why?"

"He has the missing pages to my sister's ledger."

"What makes you think Carl has them?"

"He disappeared the same time they did."

"Go through his pockets. If we can find out where he lives, you can search his place."

Leigh rushed to the body, returning with a wad of money and two keys. "One's for a car. The other looks like it'll fit a door."

"Probably a hotel room, Leigh. You can find out which one by the number stamped on the side of the key."

"How did you get the drop on Carl?"

"I instinctively released the safety and cocked the hammer before I opened the door. I lowered the gun when I recognized him, then noticed—almost too late—that he kept his right hand in his pocket."

Leigh realized she had nearly lost the man she loved. Her hands trembled as she dressed his wound. Then she sat down beside Dan, took him in her arms and cried softly. Moments later she picked up the phone.

"Paulita, can you send someone here to get rid of Carl's body? He tried to shoot Dan, but Dan beat him to the draw."

"How is your man?"

"Only a flesh wound, but it scared hell out of me."

"I'll pick up a laundry truck and be there in fifteen minutes. Did Skarlotta put out a contract on him?"

"How'd you know?"

"Miguel figured on it. His investigation had Skarlotta up to his eyeballs in laundering money for a crime family in the States. I gave a copy of the report to Dan."

"Skarlotta found out and sent his assassin," Leigh said.

"We have a leak, and I think I know who. Carl was friendly with a woman in our reserve cadre. She was at Miguel's headquarters when the report came in."

Leigh hung up, then peeked into the hall to see if the gun shot had attracted attention.

"No need to worry, Leigh. My neighbors work at night and the floor below is under repair."

"How about the people across the hall?"

"They mind their own business. Probably looked out, then went back to their TV program. Which reminds me, I've got to catch the late news report."

"What's so important about the news tonight, Dan?"

"Morales sent word to watch it."

"Okay, but do it from bed while I clean up this mess."

After helping Dan get settled, Leigh turned on the TV, then went to work. She stopped to listen when the announcer interrupted his newscast for a special bulletin.

"A U.S. military transport plane exploded shortly after take off from Guam early tonight. Rescue efforts are under way, but finding survivors is unlikely. Eyewitnesses say bits and pieces were all that remained of the plane that fell into the Pacific Ocean after the explosion. Frederik Skarlotta, Second Secretary to the U.S. Embassy in Manila, was aboard. Other names are being withheld pending notification of kin. More details will be provided as they become available."

Leigh turned off the television, looked at Dan.

"Fred made a mistake when he doctored that message to Morales about Aquino's arrival," Dan said. "Our Communist friend just took his vengeance."

"Miguel thought we could have saved Ninoy if he had had the right schedule. But my God, killing everyone on the plane to get one man is barbaric."

"That's Miguel Morales' way. Anyway, I don't have time to stay in bed."

Despite Leigh's protest, Dan got up and went to the sitting room. He helped her cover Carl's body with plastic wrap. They cleaned the carpet, then sat down to wait for Paulita. Soon, they heard a gentle knock on the door. Dressed as a maid, Paulita pushed a laundry hamper filled with sheets into the room. She tossed another maid's uniform to Leigh who slipped it on. Then they lifted Carl's body, dumped it into the hamper, covering it with soiled linen.

"I found a hotel room key in his pocket, Paulita. Do you know anyone in the police department who can find the name of the hotel from the number?"

"I know where he was staying. We'll get rid of the body, then go to his place."

Leigh kissed Dan goodbye, helped Paulita wheel the hamper to the service elevator. At ground level, they went out the hotel's rear exit to a van, put the large laundry basket in back and drove away.

"I've been thinking about Carl," Paulita said. "His family is into many criminal activities, but black-mail doesn't make sense for a hired killer."

"I don't know what to think, Paulita. Carl has to have those missing pages or I'm out of ideas."

"We can check his place, but I don't think we'll find anything. You aren't rich. Why would anyone want to black-mail you?"

"Don't say that, Paulita. Maybe Carl thought I still have the gold. Either that or someone else is his victim. How about General Navarro?"

"I don't think he'd give in to blackmail."

"Paulita, I'm confused. What if those missing pages aren't in Carl's room? Or what if they are, but don't tell me anything?"

After dumping the body in the river, Leigh and Paulita drove to Carl's hotel, entered his room. They found a suitcase filled with clothes, and an airplane ticket to New York. Leigh and Paulita tore everything apart and discovered a key to a safe deposit box in the lining of a sport coat.

"I have a friend who can find out which bank owns this key," Paulita said.

"How can we get in his safe deposit box?"

"After we find the bank, I'll get a copy of Carl's signature card, then practice my forgery."

"Oh Lord, another delay."

"Sorry, Leigh. Anyway, we located a husband and wife team who are superb mimics. And we've got recordings of voices they'll have to imitate when we attack the Palace."

"Are you trying to change the subject to get my mind off personal problems, Paulita?"

As she prepared to brief guerrilla commanders involved in the attack on Marcos' Army, Leigh still hadn't found the missing pages to her sister's ledger. Paulita stood in front of a large-scale map at Morales' Manila headquarters. Marci, Max, Jun and Revie occupied seats at an oval table. As Miguel's deputy, Leigh sat next to him.

"I've gone over details with everyone individually," Paulita said. "Now Leigh will cover the operations plan for our attack on Malacanang Palace."

Leigh stood up, took a deep breath, then started talking.

"On the day of execution, snipers from Marci's, Jun's and Revie's companies will be in position by 0130 hours. They'll cover three sides of the Palace, leaving the waterfront open. Max's snipers will cover the Pasig River. Marcos will cross it in an effort to escape."

"We'll set off mines to make sure he doesn't go down stream," Max added.

"The final change of the Palace Guard will begin at 0200 hours," Leigh continued. "Snipers with night scopes and silencers will start picking off the guards a few minutes after they go on duty. As each goes down, the sniper who kills him will notify our comm center. Paulita has a team trained to make hourly reports, imitating guards' voices."

"What about reserves?" Jun asked.

"The day before we attack, our contact at the TV station will broadcast a coded signal to activate civilian reserves. They'll be attached to each of you, putting your companies at reinforced battalion strength."

"How about logistic support?"

"Activated the same time as the reserves," Leigh replied. "Snipers will eliminate perimeter guards by 0245 hours, ignoring the main gate. It's too brightly lighted. Max's explosive platoon will plant charges at the front and side walls, setting them off at first light. That'll signal the start of a three-pronged attack: Marci going through holes in the front wall, Jun through the southwest and Revie the northeast."

"That takes care of one platoon from Max's company," Revie said. "What about the others?"

"They'll be across the river. When Marcos' party gets there, Max will capture them."

"Is the Palace communication system compromised?"

"Only the telephones," Leigh replied. "Paulita's team is prepared to imitate the voice of anyone Marcos is likely to contact. We're still trying to get Philippine Army radio frequencies."

"That leaves the operation against the Army up to three battalion commanders who support us, doesn't it?"

"Pretty much so," Miguel interrupted. "They'll move against Marcos' loyalists in the military and provide us howitzers in unmarked moving vans."

"Let's say we succeed," Jun said. "Who's going to run the government?"

"We are going to succeed," Miguel replied. "We're already in contact with opposition leaders who know nothing about our planned attack, but suspect something is brewing."

One of Paulita's intelligence officers entered. "Sorry to interrupt. Marcos just announced he'll hold an unscheduled election in three months. He was hooked up in a country to country TV broadcast with American newscasters who goaded him into making the statement."

"Stay on top of it," Leigh said.

"Well, comrades, what do you think?" Miguel asked.

Everyone started talking at the same time. Leigh put a finger to her lips. "One at at time, please. Jun, any comments?"

"I don't trust Marcos to hold a snap election. But I guess if he made the announcement on television, he has to stick to it."

"Revie, what about you?"

"He'll hold the election, then stuff the ballot boxes."

"Max?"

"Marcos will find a way to steal the election."

"What about it, Marci?" Leigh asked as Paulita left the room. "Will there be any change in our status? And will we be better off, or worse?"

"We were supposed to attack next Sunday. That's only a week away and security is already a problem. It's too risky to delay three months."

"What you have all said is correct," Miguel acknowledged. "Let's assume we wait for the election. Will opposition leaders sacrifice their own personal ambitions and unite against Marcos? Does waiting provide any advantage we don't have now? Will we have more support, or less? Marcos will win at any cost. Will his fraud become a sore point? Will fence-sitters move our way? Finally, will it sway the people to support the revolution?"

Miguel stopped talking, looked askance at Jun who smiled, nodding to hold up the attack. Revie also accepted the decision. Max started to say something, then nodded instead. Paulita returned. Miguel raised his eyebrows at Marci.

"It's worth the risk, but we must tighten security," Marci said. "I'm hesitant about our chances, but we'll have popular support if we wait. That could make a difference."

"Paulita, what did you learn?"

"The election will be held the seventh of February. Marcos agreed to let American congressmen oversee it. He's going to steal the election out from under their noses."

Miguel nodded to Leigh.

"All right, we hold," Leigh said. "Keep everything under wraps. I'll be in touch. We can get together for briefing after they count the votes."

Nodding as they rose, the commanders left. Leigh put her arm around Paulita's shoulder and walked toward an empty room down the hall.

"Can we hold the line on leaks for three months?"

"Lord knows," Paulita replied, closing the door. "We found Carl's safe deposit box."

"Were you able to get into it?"

"Not yet. We're working on it. It's going to take time, but don't get your hopes up too much, Leigh. I really don't think we're going to find anything. Why don't you talk to Miguel again? He's the last one who had that ledger."

"He makes me furious, the way he sidesteps my questions. Talking to him wouldn't accomplish anything. The only way to get Miguel to open up is to tell him I'm going to quit."

"You can't do that, Leigh. We need you."

"Not as much as I need my son."

"How about the duplicate records Marci's folks took home from Dr. Zurate's hospital?"

"Marci said she gave me everything."

"Maybe she's lying. Go to San Carlos and check it out."

"I'd rather wait until you get into Carl's safe deposit."

"You've got plenty of time now, Leigh. Think you'll find something to confirm your fears that Sumo was your son?"

"It can't be, Paulita. It just can't be."

"Then go to San Carlos."

"Okay, damn it, I'll go to San Carlos and check Marci's house."

Chapter XXXVI

Disguised as a soldier, Leigh knocked on the door of the Moreto home in San Carlos. Marci's little sister, Tina, opened it. From the expression on her face, Leigh knew the girl recognized her, but seemed afraid to acknowledge it.

"May I come in, Tina?"

"What are you doing here?" Tina whispered, stepping aside to let Leigh enter.

"Just dropped by to see how you're getting along," Leigh lied. "Are you alone?"

"Grandma went to the market with a friend. Would you like some tea?"

"Will you show me around the house first?"

Tina showed Leigh the ground floor, then led the way upstairs to the master bedroom. She pointed out the entrances to Papa's study and Mama's sewing room at the far end of the suite. Leigh strolled through the bedroom, glanced into the sewing room, then went in the study.

"Very nice, Tina. Have all the repairs been completed?"

"What repairs?"

"From the fire."

"Oh—oh—y-y-yes," Tina stammered. "It wasn't really much of a fire. Burned all the papers from the hospital."

Leigh casually opened the desk drawers, finding a folder of papers in the top one. Could these be hospital records Marci had overlooked? She lifted the cover, glanced at the top paper, then closed it. A medical report. She must take the folder with her.

"I think these are the papers Marci wanted me to pick up for her," Leigh said. "Did she say anything to you?"

"No. Are you sure?"

"That's what I asked. So you don't know if these are the right papers? Well, they must be the ones. Are there any other papers?"

"There are no others here."

"Okay, I'll take them to her." Leigh glanced at her watch. "Oh Lord, I have to get back to camp."

She had discovered Morales furious when she returned to his camp in the hills because General Ver had been acquitted in the death of Ninoy Aquino and reinstated as Marcos' Chief of Staff. Leigh worked with the other guerrilla leaders for the next three months until Morales ordered all to return to Manila and await the results of the election.

Now, as her taxi neared guerrilla headquarters in Manila, Leigh spotted a group of soldiers hiding behind a market. Her stomach churned, adding to the discomfort of an earlier attack of nausea. She took a gun from her bag, stuffed it in her waist band. Continuing to guerrilla headquarters was risky, but she must warn Paulita. When the cab stopped, Leigh jumped out, running onto the front porch. Paulita opened the door, pulled her in.

"We've been compromised, Leigh. I've been waiting for you to get here or I'd be long gone."

"What happened?"

"Marcos' Military Intelligence picked up one of the battalion commanders who supports us. They tortured him until he talked. The other battalion commanders are hiding out. They can't find them, but neither can we."

"What about our people?"

"Miguel sent word warning us. I had my staff go to our alternate headquarters. They went out the emergency escape route. Come on, let's move."

A volley of shots splintered the front door, followed by automatic rifle fire at the rear, then heavy footsteps and shouting. Leigh pulled Paulita through a room full of desks and filing cabinets. Stepping inside a closet, they pushed open a wall hinged at one end, took hold of the rungs of a ladder and struggled up into a dark cavity. Paulita's maddening slow pace grated on Leigh's nerves. She held her tongue, however, since soldiers were already tramping around in the room below. At the top, Paulita and Leigh crawled through a corrugated metal tube to an office in the next building.

"I didn't think I could make it up the ladder, and that damn tunnel played hell with my knees," Paulita said, limping across the room.

"I'm exhausted, Paulita. Don't know what's wrong with me. Maybe I picked up a flu bug."

"The stairway's at the end of the hallway to our left, Leigh. Max is waiting with a cab at the side exit."

Leigh took Paulita's arm, hustled her down the stairs to the first floor. They hurried along a corridor, dashed into the street and jumped in a taxi. Max waved from the end of the building. After glancing around the corner, he ran back to his cab.

"They must have found the ladder. Soldiers are spreading out all over the neighborhood."

"We made it in spite of my game leg. Do you have a headache, Leigh?"

"Yeah, I have a damn headache. Get to our headquarters as fast as you can, Max."

Leigh leaned back against the seat. Why had she been so abrupt? It wasn't Paulita's fault they were nearly captured. Leigh felt tired and dizzy. She closed her eyes and dozed, waking up when Max pulled into a driveway alongside a run-down building. She yawned, followed Paulita and Max inside. Paulita's intelligence staff was putting away things they brought from their abandoned headquarters. Smiling in relief, they filled paper plates with fried rice, chicken and lumpia, and started eating. Leigh poured a cup of coffee, grimacing as she sat down. She took the gun from her waist band and set it on the table, then massaged her pelvic area.

"Bring me up to date, Paulita," Leigh said, sipping the hot liquid. "I heard so many stories up-country, I don't know what to believe."

"Marcos' thugs grabbed scores of ballot boxes. They even went to the polls and paid people to vote for him like American ward heelers in the old days."

"Any comment from the American congressional committee who's overseeing the election?"

"Senator Luger said it was a fraud. Anyway, some precinct workers formed human chains and carried ballot boxes to election headquarters to keep them from being stolen."

"What good will that do? Marcos will have the figures changed before they're posted."

"Thirty computer operators walked away with copies of tally sheets that will prove Marcos is trying to steal the election."

"So that's how Corazon Aquino was able to announce at 2:00 A. M. the morning after the polls closed that she had won. Where are the computer operators now?"

"Marcos' people tried to arrest them, but they're being protected by members of Reform the Armed Forces movement."

"RAM broke with Marcos? A good sign, Paulita. Is that everything?"

"The Church will make an important announcement on the radio tonight."

"I doubt anything they say will do any good. Morales thinks the time is ripe for attack, but we still need help from the military. If we can't find the battalion commanders who went into hiding, we should talk with RAM officers. Can you arrange a meeting?"

"Miguel's on top of it."

"Did you get into Carl's safe deposit box?"

"Not yet, but we're working on it."

"Are you making any progress?"

"The safe deposit custodian's doctor is sympathetic to our cause, and he's into hypnosis. We're hoping to get him to plant a post-hypnotic suggestion in the custodian's mind to open Carl's box."

"Maybe it'll work, Paulita. Has he agreed?"

"He's wrestling with his conscience."

"I'll stick a gun barrel up his damn nose and blow his conscience to hell if he doesn't cooperate."

"Easy, Leigh, don't get pissed off. Just tell the doctor your story. He'll come around. I'll arrange a meeting."

Leigh took a deep breath, sighed. "Okay."

"Did you find anything at Marci's house?" Paulita asked.

"I picked up a few legal documents and some medical papers. I think the names have been doctored on some of the records. I don't know how to find out what the original entries were."

"I know someone who can have a look and maybe tell you what changes, if any, have been made. Did the Moretos really have a fire?"

"I'm not sure, Paulita. Could have been, but something didn't look right."

"What do you mean?"

"There was little evidence of damage. The house should look new as if it's been repaired, but it doesn't."

"Better have a heart to heart talk with Marci. First, let's see if the papers you picked up have been altered."

"Okay, Paulita. Anyway, with this headache, I don't feel like talking to Marci right now."

"And you've got to pin Miguel down. Get everything he knows. He's a stubborn son-of-a-bitch, but he realizes you're indispensable to this operation. Yell and scream, and threaten him, but don't quit on us, Leigh."

Chapter XXXVII

A few days later, Leigh awoke with an attack of nausea. She eased out of bed so as not to disturb Dan, dashed into the bathroom and vomited. Must have been something she ate last night. Still, she had been having trouble holding down breakfast since returning from her last trip up-country. She could have picked up a bug. Should see a doctor, but there was too much to do. Leigh brushed her teeth, returned to the bedroom.

Dan was sitting up in bed. "Something wrong?"

"I was wondering if you were going to sleep all day," she said, ignoring the question, sitting on the bed, running her hand through his disheveled hair. "Are you finished with your investigation? It was so late when I picked you up at the airport last night, I forgot to ask."

"It's finally over." Dan sighed, kissed her on the cheek. "I put together enough evidence to convict the top dogs in the Skarlotta family."

"What does Congressman Williams think about you spending so much time on it?"

"He fired me. I knew it was coming because he suspected I've been helping the guerrillas. How about you? Are you going to start your revolution now, or will you wait for the results of the farce Marcos calls an election?"

"As soon as we meet with RAM officers and work out details, we'll know for sure."

"Cory Aquino has called for a boycott of banks and government controlled businesses. That'll help you, but she supports Cardinal

Sin's policy of non-violence and he would consider your armed revolt a cardinal sin."

"So Cardinal Sin thinks our revolt is a cardinal sin? Funny, Dan, but he may not appreciate your play on words."

"I've heard the Cardinal has a good sense of humor. He calls his home the House of Sin."

"Maybe so. Anyway, I must get dressed and put together a briefing before we meet with RAM officers. What are you going to do now that you're out of a job?"

"I met a guy on the plane who offered to take me into his company. He's working on a sales pitch to the owners of those non-denominational churches that have sprung up all over the Philippines."

"Where does the money come from to build them?"

"Donations. The dude thinks contributions can be doubled by putting up lighted balloons of the Virgin Mary at night."

"That's disgusting," Leigh replied. "You're not going to work for that parasite, are you?"

"Don't get up-tight, Leigh, I was kidding. Actually, he was drinking heavily, and couldn't find 'EDSA Street' on his map. I pointed out Epifanio de los Santos Avenue."

"Sorry, Dan, I've been under a lot of pressure. Got to go. I'll call when I can."

As Leigh walked into guerrilla headquarters, she noticed a puzzled expression on Paulita's face.

"What's going on? Where's Marci?"

"She went to get Virgil. Things have been happening fast since you left last night to pick up Dan."

"Virgil will object to what we're planning."

"There have been major changes," Paulita continued. "We don't know what to make of them. Enrile and Ramos have broken with Marcos. They're holed up in Camp Aguinaldo and Camp Crame with RAM supporters."

"The Defense Minister and the Deputy Chief of Staff? I can't believe it. Why?"

"Marcos was getting ready to arrest them."

"Hmmm. Why is Virgil coming here?"

"He's guessed we're ready to kick off our operation and has something important to discuss with us."

Morales entered the room. "That's the same peaceful protest crap Cardinal Sin and Cory Aquino have been pushing. It'll get everyone killed. Marcos would love an excuse to order his soldiers to shoot into the crowd."

"Let's listen to what Virgil has to say," Leigh said.

"We can do that, but I'm not accepting anything on blind faith. Come to think of it, it might be to our benefit if soldiers did shoot the protesters."

"You want them to kill innocent people?"

"I don't want anyone killed, but we must take advantage of every opportunity that comes our way. Most people who turn the other cheek will eventually fight. We must be ready to accept friends and relatives of those who're shot."

A car drove up alongside the building. Paulita opened the door so Marci could push Virgil into the room. Leigh removed a bandana covering his eyes, then hugged him.

"Sorry about the blindfold, Virgil, but Miguel insisted on it since our last headquarters were compromised."

"It's okay, Auntie Leigh," Virgil said when his eyes had adjusted to the light. "Miguel, if you'll hold off your attack until our demonstration in support of Enrile and Ramos has had a chance to succeed, I'll make it worth while."

"What do you have to offer?"

"I'll put you in touch with the Philippine Army officers who hid out when Marcos' people picked up that battalion commander who sold you down the river when interrogators put the pressure on him. The other two commanders have given us radio frequencies and a code book. And they've set up a communications center for us."

"We can't wait," Morales said. "RAM officers will be killed if we don't move quickly. We owe them nothing, but we do need their contacts. The Army officers you're hiding are important, but they can't swing as much support as Reform the Armed Forces Movement."

"Seminaries and convents all over Metro-Manila, including priests, nuns and Cory's followers, are effectively organized for demonstrations. We're putting out another appeal, and more people will respond. The streets will be filled with protesters."

"We'll kill innocent people if we attack now, Miguel," Leigh said. "If Virgil is willing to give us something, we can delay execution without serious harm to our plans."

Morales lit a cigar. "I'm listening."

"Put us in contact with the Army officers now, Virgil," Leigh said. "And give us access to your comm center."

"Okay, we can handle that. Is that it?"

"Not entirely. We'll decide when your demonstration has succeeded or failed."

"You can't do that from here, Auntie Leigh."

"I'll be with you," she replied.

"I'll buy that," Miguel said. "Leigh, you and Max go with Virgil to be sure we get what we've bargained for."

"Okay, I agree. But I'm depending on you, Auntie Leigh, to give us a reasonable chance."

Chapter XXXVIII

An hour before dawn, Leigh rose from her chair, yawning as she stretched. Hours of listening to Philippine Army radio frequencies brought no information on troop movements. The brother of the late Ninoy Aquino had broadcast an appeal on Radio Veritas for mass demonstrations. Cardinal Sin requested that priests and nuns pray for Enrile, Ramos and supporters.

"Max, let's go to Camp Crame and see what's going on," Leigh said. "We're not getting the full story here. Maybe we're tuned to the wrong radio frequencies."

"Yeah, the Army probably changed them. Is that where Virgil went?"

"He sneaked away when I wasn't looking, but I'll bet that's where we'll find him. I want to be with him when all hell breaks loose."

They drove down a side street, then onto EDSA and headed for Camp Crame. People were straggling away from what was to have been a confrontation between unarmed Filipinos and Marcos' soldiers. Leigh nodded. At least innocent civilians wouldn't be killed when the military arrived. And they would come, probably right after sunrise. Leigh surveyed the route as they drove along. Now that the protesters were out of the way, Miguel would want her to pick out spots to ambush the soldiers who attack the camps. Near the main gate to Camp Crame, a hundred demonstrators remained. Virgil wheeled himself to their cab.

"Is this what you meant when you said the streets would be filled with demonstrators, Virgil?"

"They'll be back, Auntie Leigh. Marcos didn't attack because he's afraid to go up against the Church."

"The Army is probably cranking up the engines on tanks and armored personnel carriers right now. Marcos will kill these demonstrators, then convince the world there was a coup attempt started by Communist conspirators. And he'll get away with it."

"We know the Army will come, probably after the noon Mass," Virgil said. "General Ver will likely call his commanders this morning to give the order. Paulita will intercept the message, then let me know where they're going to breach Camp Crame and Camp Aguinaldo. And we'll move our people to cover those spots."

"I have a feeling they're going to attack at dawn, and that isn't far off. I've waited as long as I can, Virgil. All your demonstrators, except a few diehards, are gone."

"Some are only taking a rest. The others went after tools and equipment, and they're on the way back right now to put up barricades."

As Virgil wheeled away, Leigh shook her head. It was useless to argue with her strong-willed nephew. She knew the demonstration had failed, and so did he.

"Max, he's going to be killed. We don't have much time. Let's grab Virgil and get him out of the way before the Army arrives."

"Yeah, the sun's about ready to come up. Hey, what's that rumbling?"

Leigh cocked her ear. Laboring engines. Oh Lord, heavy vehicles were moving along EDSA. The rumbling was drowned out by loud noises like trees and telephone poles crashing to the ground. My God, tanks were coming.

Chapter XXXIX

"Virgil!" Leigh screamed.

"Take it easy, Auntie Leigh. Trucks are bringing our people back with tools and supplies."

"What kind of tools and supplies?"

"Sand, shovels, empty gunny sacks, saws, axes. They're felling trees for barricades right now."

"Perhaps we were a bit hasty, Max. Come on, let's have a look around."

"Give me your word you won't bring the guerrillas until we've had a chance to stop the Philippine Army without violence," Virgil said.

"We have to move our people close enough so they can react quickly, Virgil. And we must position snipers to pick off Army artillerymen when they bring howitzers."

"Where will you be?" Virgil asked. "I want your word you'll let me know when Miguel orders an attack."

"As soon as we're set up, I'll come back and stick with you," Leigh replied.

"Don't bring weapons. We won't be armed, but if some hot-head gets hold of a gun, Lord knows what'll happen."

"Max, let's get out of here while I still have some sanity left."

As the sun peeked over the horizon, Leigh and Max drove away. Groups of protesters were constructing barricades across ten-lane wide EDSA, using sandbags, drainage grills, lamp posts and any-thing else they could get their hands on. On side streets, they were cutting down trees, then dragging them across the narrow passage-ways, blocking entrance to the busy thoroughfare.

"People are better organized than we thought, Max."

"Yeah, but their barricades ain't worth a damn against armored vehicles."

"Stop here. I want to mark some spots on the map where we should put our troops."

Max pulled up to the curb, waited a few moments, then handed Leigh his radio.

"Legs, this is Nightingale, over," Leigh radioed to guerrilla head-quarters.

"Dan has been trying to reach you," Paulita replied.

"I'll call him as soon as I find a phone. I have to get in the building Marci's family owns on EDSA," Leigh said.

"She's here now, just a moment." After a pause, Paulita contin-ued. "She says she can get hold of her cousin and be there in an hour."

"Good. I'm working on a dispersement plan for M&M," Leigh said, using Miguel Morales' code name. "Max will deliver it after he drops me off."

"The Moreto Medical Building is behind us, Leigh," Max said. "Want to turn around?"

"Take a side street, then go around Camp Aguinaldo and back to EDSA along the north wall of Camp Crame."

As they circled the camps, Leigh realized the appeal by Cardinal Sin to protect the rebels had taken root. People arrived on foot, and by car and bus. Women brought food, passing it over the fence to soldiers supporting RAM rebels inside the compounds. Nuns pre-pared meals on portable stoves, and that, too, went to the rebels. Statues of the Virgin Mother, held over the heads of the crowd, seemed to float like balloons above the surging mass. An idea began to take shape in her mind. Leigh smiled.

"Leigh, I can't get any closer," Max shouted.

"I'll walk from here, Max. Have Miguel set up snipers and deploy the troops as I've marked on the map. Tell him not to attack until I work out something with Dan."

"How does Dan fit into this?"

"Maybe he doesn't, but seeing those statues of the Virgin Mother reminded me of something."

Fifteen minutes later, Leigh squeezed through the crowd to the entrance of a five-story medical building. Marci was waiting in the lobby with another woman.

"Leigh, this is my cousin, Dr. Sonia Moreto. Her office is on the top floor overlooking EDSA."

They took an elevator to a fifth floor office. Leigh plopped down in a chair, picked up the phone.

"Dan, can you meet me at the Moreto Medical Building on EDSA?"

"Are you all right, Leigh?"

"I'm fine, but I need a change of clothes. Bring the suitcase next to the couch in the sitting room."

"I'll be there as soon as I can," Dan replied.

When Leigh hung up, Marci said, "Sonia has set up a mobile clinic for demonstrators, but she'll support us."

"I will if you give the demonstration a chance to succeed before you do anything," Dr. Moreto said.

"There are so many people, I think the Philippine Army will come only for a show of force today," Leigh replied. "Marcos must realize he can't kill everyone without bringing reprisals from around the world."

"If he holds off today, shouldn't we go ahead with our original attack plan?" Marci asked.

"That's what I was thinking, except for a few changes. We'll use half the snipers here in support of the rebels in Camp Crame and the other half at the Palace."

"I've got to get back to my company, Leigh."

"Turn command over to your deputy, then come back here with a skeleton staff and set up another headquarters. Miguel will okay it when I tell him what I have in mind. I want to put our special platoons under you as commander of a new company in support of the rebels."

"Where will you be?" Marci asked.

"With Virgil. I'll keep in touch by radio. Our major effort will be here. It should convince RAM officers to throw in with us. With their support in the military, we have a chance of making this work."

"I'm on my way, Leigh. Why not have Sonia check your eye while you're waiting for Dan?"

Leigh nodded, then noticed that Marci made no effort to move. "I want to talk to you too, but not now. Anything else that has to be discussed at this moment?"

Marci shook her head, dashed out the door.

After taking off Leigh's eye patch, Dr. Moreto said, "I think it's coming along nicely. See an ophthalmologist as soon as you can, to be sure. In the meantime, wear sun glasses. You don't look well, Leigh. Why don't I give you a physical examination while we're waiting?"

"I don't have time."

"At least let me take a blood sample and urinalysis."

As they finished the tests, Dan arrived with Leigh's suitcase.

"Sorry it took so long, but I've never seen anything like this. You should know the U.S. Ambassador advised Marcos not to harm the demonstrators."

"I'm counting on it for today. Can you get hold of that dude with balloons of the Virgin Mother?"

"What the hell do you want with him?" Dan asked.

"Not him—his balloons. Marcos will probably send troops here this afternoon to frighten the people, then back off until morning. I want you to put balloons up over the soldiers' campsites tonight."

"You want me to fly balloons over their camps tonight? Come on, get realistic."

"My nephew's with the demonstrators," Leigh replied. "I must do everything possible to keep him alive, no matter how unrealistic. Filipino soldiers are devout Catholics. I want to give them something to think about. Maybe they'll believe they're experiencing a religious miracle."

"Okay, let me know where they set up camp. I suppose you'd like to attach a tape recorder to those floating images and send a spiritual message to the troops."

"Not a bad idea. Did I see a music studio on the first floor, Sonia?"

"My sister's place. She's with the demonstrators. I'll let you in."

"Take Dan down and record a message while I work out details of our plan. Something simple like, 'Soldiers, in the name of God, don't kill your own people.' Perhaps some religious organ music in the background."

Chapter XXXX

Dressed in slacks, yellow blouse, baseball cap and sun glasses, Leigh struggled through the crowd. She spotted a group of white-robed seminarians headed the way she wanted to go and fell in behind them. A man with an ornate image of the Virgin Mary atop his head came up beside her.

"Minister Enrile left Camp Aguinaldo and has joined General Ramos at Camp Crame," he said.

"Have any military units defected?" Leigh asked.

"Enrile and Ramos have been calling their friends, but they're all waiting to see what happens."

"What is the Philippine Army doing?" Leigh asked.

"General Ver is moving combat units onto EDSA. The seminarians are headed there."

That's where Virgil would be, right in the thick of the action. Leigh stayed behind the religious brothers. It took an hour to cover the two kilometers to Ortigas Avenue. Tanks and armored personnel carriers—dwarfing demonstrators standing in their path—had already reached the intersection. Marines with bandoleers of ammunition across their shoulders climbed down, then stood stoically between armored vehicles and demonstrators. Virgil was with a group of nuns on their knees, praying the Rosary into the ears of stone-faced military men.

Leigh took out her radio. "Legs, this is Nightingale, over."

"Where are you?" Paulita replied.

"I'm at the intersection of EDSA and Ortigas Avenue."

"Then you know what's happening. Anyway, you were right about the documents you picked up from Marci's house. They have been altered. Want to know how?"

Someone jostled the radio out of Leigh's hands. She stooped to pick it up. It was swept away under the feet of worshipers. Leigh sighed. Now how would she contact Paulita?

First, she must think about Virgil. If she could get across the street, maybe she could grab his wheel chair and push him out of the way. Leigh sidled around an armored personnel carrier. Young women with flowers moved among marines. Some accepted bouquets thrust at them. That tiny flaw in their military armor of resolve gave Leigh a glimmer of hope. She reached the praying nuns, but could get no closer to Virgil.

The commanding general came to the front of the column. His face showed he was agonizing over his duty to superiors and reluctance to run over innocent men, women and children. Would he attack? Leigh shook her head.

"Lord, I hope I'm right," she mumbled.

In the late afternoon, marines returned to their vehicles. What were they going to do now? Engines roared to life. People moved forward, placed their hands on the tanks, pushing futilely. Armored cars surged forward. Men and women backed away, then dropped to their knees. Virgil shoved out of his wheel chair, prostrating himself in front of a tank.

Leigh called to her nephew, but couldn't attract his attention. She tried to squeeze through the nuns. They refused to budge. She was trapped. No chance of moving nearer to Virgil. Was there another way to get him away from this confrontation? She could think of nothing. Overwhelmed with helplessness, Leigh, too, dropped onto her knees. She took out her rosary beads, clutched them to her breast and looked into the heavens.

Chapter XXXXI

Black smoke billowed from tank exhausts. The pungent odor of carbon monoxide made Leigh dizzy. Protesters, who crowded around her, dropped to their knees, fingering rosary beads. Others sat cross-legged or, like Virgil, lay prostrate in front of monstrous armored vehicles. Tears, mingling with perspiration, soaked their clothes. Leigh shook her head. Why was she with these idiots? To get Virgil out of harm's way, but that was impossible.

"Oh God, this is really stupid," she mumbled.

Engines roaring, tanks jerked forward. Gasping in fear, demonstrators determinedly held their ground. Leigh prayed no one would panic. Being trampled by a terror-stricken mob was something she didn't relish. Still, that couldn't be any worse than getting crushed under tank treads. If only she hadn't lost her radio, she could have called guerrilla anti-tank gunners. There would have been friendly casualties, but not the massacre that was about to unfold.

Next to Leigh, a kneeling seminarian pulled out a two-way radio. This could be her answer. Leigh grabbed it. "Let me have that."

She changed frequencies, ignoring the look of protest on the brother's face. His dismay reminded Leigh of her promise to Virgil. Had she really allowed the demonstrators enough time? Treads clanked as armored vehicles started forward. That was her answer. No question about it. They were going to run everyone down. She must call the anti-tank gunners. Hands trembling, Leigh pressed the transmitter button. The tanks stopped. She hesitated. The driver in front of her revved up his engine, jammed the tank into gear. Intuition made Leigh hold the call.

Suddenly, the armored vehicles backed away. A hushed silence fell over the crowd. Cheers rose from their throats as the military vehicles continued to retreat. Tears of relief filled Leigh's eyes. She realized this was only a temporary reprieve, but, fortunately, she had been right. Marcos' troops had been putting on a show of force. And it had been damn effective.

"Sorry about the radio," Leigh said, returning it to the seminarian.

Leigh sighed. Her body ached from tension, exhaustion and frayed nerves. She looked around. She wasn't the only one suffering the effects. Pain was etched on every face. Some demonstrators cried. Others shouted for joy. Had their resolve to block Marcos' troops been eroded by this traumatic experience? They were jumping for joy now, hugging and kissing each other, not even thinking about tomorrow. When the tanks returned, people would run. Some would fall and be trampled by those behind. If they held their ground, tanks would crush them. She shook her head. Finally able to squeeze through the crowd, Leigh hurried to Virgil.

"It isn't over, Virgil, they'll be back."

"And we'll be here. The tanks didn't run us down. They retreated because the generals realized we would hold the line no matter what."

"You're hopeless."

"Have you lost your faith in God, Auntie Leigh?"

"Nightingale, this is Legs," a voice on Virgil's radio said. "Come in, Nightingale. What's going on?"

"Sounds like Paulita on my frequency." Virgil handed his radio to Leigh.

"The tanks have backed off for the night," Leigh radioed. "I'm sure they'll return at first light."

"So we heard. M&M wants to take them out now that they've moved away from the people."

"No, you can't," Virgil said.

"Hold on, Legs." Leigh stared at her nephew, then sighed. "Virgil, Marcos' soldiers will return tomorrow, and they won't stop with a show of force."

"We made them back off without firing a shot. You can't attack as long as they only threaten us. You promised."

"All right, damn it. I'll try to convince Miguel he must give your demonstration more time. But you have to stay out of the front ranks."

"Don't you understand what happened?" Virgil asked. "Unwavering Filipina courage won this battle. Nuns were on the front lines. Soldiers can't kill women, and cripples like me. I was so hyped up, I thought I felt a tingling in my legs. It's gone now that I realize what's ahead of us."

"Virgil, we can't hold off until they kill all of you. When soldiers get a taste of blood, they can't stop. And fear of disobeying orders will force them to take that first taste. The moment they run over one demonstrator, we start shooting."

"Don't do it, no matter what."

Leigh spoke to Paulita on the radio. "I'm coming in to talk strategy with M&M. And I want to see you about Marci's altered medical papers."

"We're passing up a chance we won't get again," Paulita replied. "By the way, Dan says he's ready."

"On second thought, I'll check encampments first. I'll meet you and Dan at Marci's headquarters in two hours."

When Leigh signed off, Virgil took the radio and spoke to his supporters.

"We'll know in a few minutes where the soldiers are camped. Auntie Leigh, you look beat. Better get some rest."

Chapter XXXXII

The next morning, Leigh rubbed her eyes, got off the medical examining table where she had slept. She put on her shoes and went to the outer office as Paulita hung up the phone.

"Did you pin Miguel down last night?" Paulita asked.

"I finally got a straight answer," Leigh replied. "He was one of the four born to an unwed mother in Dr. Zurate's hospital."

"So that's why he's been holding out. Any chance you could be his mother?"

"He suspects the possibility, but doesn't want to admit it, even to himself. I don't know what to think."

"I have some things to discuss with you, but I better brief you on what's happening first."

"Okay, Paulita, what's up?"

"People are gathering along EDSA again despite the scare they got yesterday."

"Anything on the movement of armored vehicles?"

"We have reports of troops headed toward Camp Aguinaldo, and an armored column coming out of Fort Bonifacio."

"Is the armored column moving down EDSA?" Leigh asked.

"Yeah, but they haven't run over anyone. Probably hesitating because nuns are in the front ranks."

"And Virgil's with them. I've got to find a way to get him out of there. Anything else, Paulita?"

"I'm sorry, Leigh, I didn't want to tell you. The Army picked up Dan. They're holding him at Fort Bonifacio."

"Damn, I shouldn't have told him to fly those balloons over that top-security place."

"And Miguel is getting itchy. I convinced him not to attack unless the tanks actually run over demonstrators."

"Thanks, Paulita. Maybe I can get Virgil away from the demonstration if I tell him I need help in springing Dan."

"Will that be any safer than where he is?"

"It will be if we make the rescue a sneaky operation. I want to talk to Marci about those papers I picked up at her house. I was too tired to wait for her to get back last night. Where is she now?"

"On the way in with Dr. Moreto who has the results of your blood test."

"Hmm, I just thought of a way to get Dan out of Fort Bonifacio. Got to think about it a little more. Get hold of Max and have him hand-pick a squad of former soldiers. As soon as I talk to Marci, we can have a go at it."

When Dr. Sonia Moreto and Marci arrived, the doctor took Leigh's arm, led her into a private office.

"Sit down, Leigh. I have something to tell you that may come as a shock."

What did the doctor have to say? Leigh breathed deeply to steel herself for bad news.

"You're pregnant."

Leigh's mouth gaped. What Dr. Moreto had said wasn't possible, was it? Leigh struggled for words to express her feelings of dismay.

"I-I-I thought I couldn't have any more children. Are you sure, Dr. Moreto?"

"Of course I'm certain. I'm surprised you didn't know."

"I should have, but I've had so many false alarms. How far along am I? Two or three months?"

"We'll know for sure after a thorough physical exam."

Could Dr. Moreto be right? Was it possible, after all the medical specialists she had seen when she was married to Alex? Wiping tears from her eyes, Leigh looked into Sonia's smiling face. That was her answer. She sighed, slumped back in the chair. Thoughts of her son flooded into her mind. How she had felt when she was three months pregnant with him. Of going to Dr. Zurate's hospital in the hills to keep the neighbors from finding out. Swollen feet, backache and other distant memories of pain in the joy of having a baby.

"You must have a complete physical, Leigh. The life you lead isn't suited to your condition."

Oh Lord, the baby's father was a prisoner. She had to get Dan out of that horrible place. My God, everything was piling up. She must think about the idea she had mentioned to Paulita. Even as Leigh talked to Sonia, a plan to rescue Dan took shape in her mind. There was a way that might also convince Virgil he was essential to the operation.

"I intend to have a healthy child," Leigh replied. "And I'll do whatever you say after we spring Dan Hanks from Fort Bonifacio."

"Marci can work on it while I examine you."

"Let me talk to her."

Moments after Sonia left, Marci entered the office. "I'm really happy for you, Leigh. Paulita told me Dan was being held in Fort Bonifacio. First Carl tries to kill him. Now this. He has a way of attracting trouble."

"How did you know about Carl?"

"I heard someone talking about it. Oh, did you find your sister's diary?"

"There are some pages missing, Marci. Know anything about them? You said diary again. Unless you read the thing, you should think of it as Rosa's household ledger, as I have repeatedly called it."

"What are you saying, Leigh?"

"I think you got the ledger from the Sobels in Hong Kong, then surrendered it to Miguel."

"Why would I do that? It doesn't make sense, Leigh."

"I know you're lying because Miguel finally admitted you gave it to him."

"That son-of-a-bitch."

"That's true, but I had him by the balls. He was forced to tell me. You read the diary, then cut out those pages, didn't you? Why?"

"No, I didn't cut them out. It was the Sobels, or Carl."

"But you know something important. What is it, Marci? Spit it out."

"Yes, but I'm not going to tell you until you leave Virgil alone."

"I've got to get him away from those stupid demonstrators before tanks run over him. Convincing him I need his help to get Dan out of prison is the only way I can think of to keep Virgil alive."

"You can't be certain of that. The rescue could get him killed."

"We aren't going to shoot our way out of Fort Bonifacio. I have a plan that'll give us a good chance of success."

"I don't know what to think. Tell me about your fool-proof plan."

"Tell me what you know first, then I'll let you in on my plan to get Dan out of Fort Bonifacio."

"Not until Virgil returns in one piece from your rescue mission."

Marci was stubborn. And time was critical. The longer they waited, the greater the risk. Leigh shook her head in disgust.

"Okay, damn it, here's the plan."

Leigh briefed Marci, then gave her instructions to help carry it out. Marci picked up the phone as Leigh went to Dr. Moreto's examining room.

Chapter XXXXIII

Their hands bound loosely so little effort would be required to throw off the ropes, Leigh and Virgil sat in back of a military van. She had strapped an automatic pistol and bayonet to her thighs under a long skirt. He had refused a weapon. Six guerrillas, disguised as soldiers, occupied the other seats. Max, dressed in a Philippine Army officer's uniform, rode in front next to the driver. He, too, had strapped automatic pistols to each calf, under pants legs. In addition, he carried a side-arm in plain sight.

"I didn't think I would ever agree to anything like this, Auntie Leigh," Virgil said. "Marci threw me for a loop when she told me about your baby."

"Your friends will get along without you. I can't."

"We're coming to the main gate, Leigh," Max said.

"Heard anything from Paulita on the radio?"

"She said a column of tanks drove up to demonstrators on Katipunan. When women moved to the front, the tanks stopped. Soldiers refused orders to open fire. They said the Virgin Mother appeared to them last night and told them not to shoot innocent Filipinos. Can you believe it?"

"Well, I'll be damned. Dan's balloons did some good after all," Leigh replied.

Guards waved them through Fort Bonifacio's main gate, making only a cursory check of identification cards. Leigh breathed easier. Security wasn't as tight as she had expected. Still, the hard part was ahead of them. The van stopped in front of the prison compound. Leigh got out, waited with Max as two disguised guerrillas lifted

Virgil—seated in his wheel chair—and carried him into the building.

"I'm Lieutenant Garcia," Max said to the desk sergeant. "Brought
these prisoners in for General Navarro."

"He's in the interrogation room, but doesn't want anyone to disturb him."

"He'll want to know about these two."

"What's so special about the tall woman and a seminarian in a
wheel chair?"

"Don't you recognize Colonel Nightingale?" Max asked rhetori-
cally. "The crippled seminarian is wanted as an escaped Communist
guerrilla. The General had my ass for letting him get away a couple
of years ago. Now I'm going to deliver them personally and no one
is going to stop me."

"In the interrogation room on the lower floor, but you can't take
weapons down there."

"I don't need a weapon. I'll leave my side-arm here with my
troops," Max said, laying his pistol on the sergeant's desk.

"Okay, Lieutenant. Perez will go with you to push the prisoner
in the wheel chair so you can keep your eyes on Colonel Nightingale."

Max and Leigh followed Perez as he eased Virgil's wheel chair
down the stairs, then into the interrogation room. Leigh shuddered.
Dan was hanging from the ceiling, his back crisscrossed with welts
and open wounds. General Navarro stood in front of him, two soldiers, with cat-o-nine tails, on each side. The soldiers threw down
their whips, grabbed rifles that leaned against the wall.

"We meet again, Mrs. Jackson," the General said. "Or should I
call you Colonel Nightingale? I'm also pleased to see that your
nephew has come with you."

"Marcos is on his last legs, General," Leigh said. "Why are you
still operating as if he'll be in business forever?"

Leigh sidled away from Virgil. As she expected, one of the soldiers kept her under guard. When Max moved in the opposite direction, the second soldier turned toward him. She hadn't anticipated

this. That was a mistake. Concern for Dan had clouded her judgment. Virgil should have been the key to this operation, not Max. If only her nephew hadn't refused a weapon.

Leigh chewed her lip, wrestling with conflicting thoughts. Virgil suddenly wheeled backward, forcing the soldier, Perez, against the wall. As they struggled, Dan kicked away from the opposite wall. Swinging back he wrapped his legs around the neck of the soldier guarding Leigh.

As Virgil and Dan struggled with the two soldiers, Leigh threw off her ropes. She grabbed the pistol from under her skirt, fired hurriedly at the third soldier who guarded Max. Her bullet whizzed by his head, ricocheted eerily around the room. Ignoring Max, the soldier turned to confront Leigh. She dropped to the floor and rolled. Coming up on one knee, she aimed quickly and squeezed the trigger. Her bullet hit the soldier in the shoulder. He slumped to the floor.

General Navarro grabbed his gun, danced around, shifting his aim back and forth, seemingly uncertain what to do. At that moment, the first soldier wrestled free of Dan's legs. As he fired at Leigh, Dan kicked him in the back. His bullet whizzed by her head, ricocheted off the metal door, then thudded into General Navarro's stomach. A scream stuck in his throat. Blood spewing from his mouth, the General collapsed.

Max pulled out his gun, shot the soldier. Clutching his chest, he fell to the floor.

Perez, struggling with Virgil, pushed the wheel chair away from the wall, Virgil grabbed the back of Perez's jacket, hefted, then threw him over his head. Stunned, the soldier, nonetheless, crawled to the General's gun. Virgil wheeled forward and threw himself on the man. Wrenching the pistol from his hand, he smashed his fist into Perez's jaw. Max tied and gagged the unconscious soldier.

Leigh ran to a storage battery sitting against the wall, pushed it under Dan, then stepped up on it to cut him loose.

"We couldn't have pulled this off without the diversion you and Virgil started," she gasped.

"It took everything I had left in me," Dan replied.

Leigh tore off her half-slip, wrapped it loosely over his wounds. As she helped Dan to the door, Virgil yelled. Leigh rushed to her nephew. As he massaged his legs, Virgil whooped for joy, then suddenly clenched his teeth.

"What's wrong, Virgil?"

"My legs were tingling, then suddenly it felt like pins and needles jabbing into them clear down to my toes. And the feeling wasn't my imagination."

Leigh hugged Virgil, then helped Max lift him into his wheel chair as Dan looked into the corridor.

"All clear, Leigh."

"Max, call your squad leader and tell him to get the drop on the sergeant and anyone else wandering around up there," Leigh said.

She stared at General Navarro's twisted blood-soaked body, contorted face, unseeing eyes. He would give her no more trouble. As they left the torture chamber, Leigh shuddered again.

The rescuers hurried to the van and sped away. Though Leigh had expected someone would set off an alarm, none came as they neared the main gate. The sentries waved them through, their attention riveted to a news report on the radio. Leigh was momentarily engulfed in a feeling of ecstasy. The man she loved was alive, the new life within her—his baby—was safe, and Virgil's legs were also tingling with life. Thoughts of her son resurfaced, erasing everything else from her mind. Where was he? Maybe the stillborn child was hers after all. No, Rosa had said her son was alive. She wouldn't lie about that, would she? Maybe Miguel was her son? Or Sumo? No, it had to be someone else.

Chapter XXXXIV

When they arrived at guerrilla sub-headquarters it bustled with excitement at the rescue. Max helped Dan to an examination room so Dr. Moreto could treat him.

Marci hugged Virgil. "I was sitting on pins and needles waiting to hear from you. Why didn't you call?"

"I was so hyped up about the feeling in my legs, I forgot," Virgil replied.

"Oh, Virgil, I'm so happy for you," Marci said.

Leigh started massaging one of Virgil's legs. "Work on the other one, Marci. It will help circulation."

Virgil kept his silence for only a moment. "I know you and Mama didn't get along, Auntie Leigh. I don't know what started it, but she blamed herself."

"It wasn't her fault, Virgil. It was mine."

"I wish you had had a chance to resolve your differences before she died."

"Oh, we had a nice long talk on the telephone. That's why I came back to the Philippines. And to see my favorite nephew," Leigh lied, giving his beard an affectionate tug.

Dr. Moreto came out of the examining room. "Mr. Hanks took a terrible beating, but nothing is broken. He tells me your legs have been showing signs of life, Virgil."

"Yes. They feel like they've been asleep. Is that a good sign?"

"Of course. I called a neurologist who can see you now. If you're up to it, I can take you to his office."

"Let's go. See you later, Marci, Auntie Leigh."

After they left, Leigh nodded to Paulita, then dragged Marci into a vacant office to get away from the others. Paulita positioned herself outside the door to make sure they weren't disturbed.

"Marci, if you didn't cut out those pages from Rosa's ledger, what have you been holding back?"

"When I said I didn't do it, that wasn't entirely the truth, Leigh."

"So you were the one, after all?"

"No. Carl cut out most of the pages. I paid him for those, but I think he held back a few. We'll never know for sure now that he's dead. Anyway, I cut out two more pages before I gave you the diary."

"Why?"

"I was afraid to let you see them."

"Damn it, Marci, what did Rosa write that was so important?"

"When I was seven years old, my parents adopted my sister. That made me suspicious that I was also adopted. So I rummaged through their records and learned the truth."

"What does that have to do with my child?"

"I'm coming to that. The birth record showed I was born the same day as Virgil."

"What are you saying?"

"I was angry and confused. I kept it to myself for six years. Finally, I talked to my parents. They told me I was born to a woman who had been raped."

"Are you telling me you're my daughter?"

"Oh no. My birth mother died when I was born. What I'm saying is it's an awful feeling to be the off-spring of a rapist. I even thought of suicide, but faith in the Church kept me from it."

"Get to the point, Marci."

"My adopted parents told me about Virgil's birth. With everything else, I can imagine how he would feel if he found out how he was conceived."

Leigh closed her eyes, grasped the arms of a chair and slumped into it.

"Virgil is my son?" she whispered.

"Yes."

Thank God. At last she had found him. But what would he think? Leigh wiped her eyes on a handkerchief, blew her nose, then glared at Marci.

"Why didn't you want me to know?"

"Virgil loved Raul and Rosa, and he thinks they were his birth mother and father. If he finds out his real birth mother—you—was raped by the man who murdered the woman he believes was his birth mother, it will tear him apart."

"Okay, so you have what you thought was a good reason. But the decision to tell or not to tell Virgil is mine, not yours. Rosa was pregnant. What happened to her baby?"

"She and Raul had an accident on the way to the hospital and the baby was stillborn. Raul convinced the head nurse, who adopted me when my birth mother died, to make the substitution with your baby and change hospital records. They even prepared a fake death certificate."

"They stole my son!"

"I know, but please, Leigh, don't tell Virgil."

"My God, Marci, what do you want from me?"

"Think of Virgil."

"Okay, damn it, I'll consider it. Why did Carl want those pages in the first place?"

"I think Rosa accused General Fidel Navarro of raping you. Those are probably the pages Carl held back. Anyway, the General was widely known as a womanizer, but he wouldn't have wanted the word getting out he was a rapist."

Unsteadily, Leigh walked away, entering the examining room where Dan was sleeping. Could she tell Virgil she was his birth mother? And how could she let Dan know about their unborn child? Leigh lay down and slept restlessly, waking when Virgil called the next morning.

"The neurologist says the bullet has moved far enough away from my spine so they can operate, Auntie Leigh."

"Oh, Virgil, I'm so happy for you," she replied.

"I only have a hazy memory of what happened after I was shot. I don't think I could use my arms when I regained consciousness. The doctor says the bullet moved farther away from my spinal column, not closer because of what Marcos' interrogators did to me."

"You'd have had little hope of recovery if it had been the other way around. What else does your neurologist say?"

"The fight with that soldier in the torture chamber may have caused it to move a little bit more. He can operate safely now, Auntie Leigh. It's a miracle. I'll be able to walk again."

"Yes it is, Darling. That's how I feel about my baby. I'm so happy for all these little miracles. I'll be over to see you this afternoon. Bye."

Paulita came up to Leigh and whispered in her ear. "We have unfinished business at the bank."

Chapter XXXXV

As Max drove them to the Bank of the Philippines, Leigh questioned Paulita.

"I thought the bank was closed."

"Our man, Johnny, will open up early as a favor to his doctor, but he thinks we'll be going to my safe deposit."

"What must you do to get in Carl's box?"

"First, I mention Dr. Atendido's name. Then I give him a post hypnotic suggestion."

"I'm not sure this is necessary, Paulita. Marci got most of the missing pages from Carl. She destroyed them, but she told me what I needed to know."

"I heard. She thinks Carl may have held out some pages, but Marci doesn't know we're about to get in his safe deposit box. There's the bank. Pull up to the curb, Max."

"Is that Johnny—the chunky middle-aged man?"

"That's him. Let me do the talking."

When Max dropped them off, Leigh followed Paulita to the bank entrance.

"You're right on time, Johnny," Paulita said. "Dr. Atendido said you would be prompt."

"Yes, I am always on time," the man replied, waiting as though expecting instructions.

"Open up, Johnny Reb, or the Blue Bellies will get us," Paulita said.

Johnny unlocked the door, let them enter, then locked the door. He led the way downstairs, pushed a registration book in front of

Paulita. When she signed, he compared the signature with one on file for Carl, the lessee of box 339. Then he led them to the safe deposit box area.

Johnny inserted his key into the slot on Carl's box, waited until Paulita had inserted her key. Unlocking the box, he extracted it, carried it to an enclosed booth, and left them alone. Paulita opened the lid.

"My God, look at all those greenbacks! And here are the papers Carl held back." Paulita handed five notebook pages to Leigh, then stuffed the American dollars in her pack. "Let's get out of here."

Minutes later, they headed back to guerrilla headquarters in Max's taxi. Leigh read the first page.

"Listen to this entry dated the day Virgil was born. 'I was worried sick something had happened to my child because of our automobile accident, but I'm so happy for the birth of a healthy baby boy.' Marci told me Rosa's baby was stillborn as a result of that accident."

"What's it all about, Leigh?"

Ignoring the question, Leigh went back to the remaining pages. In another entry, dated a few days later, Rosa had pangs of conscience for the way she had treated her younger sister. She confessed to seeing Leigh raped, then denying it to everyone, including herself. Of how she had walked in on Fidel Navarro raping Leigh. Her anger and shame, and the traumatic feeling that clouded her good judgment. Finally, of going back to bed, trying to erase everything she'd seen from her mind.

Leigh frowned, shaking her head as she finished reading the missing pages. Finally, she looked up.

"What'd you find?" Paulita asked. "Is Virgil your son as Marci said, or isn't he?"

"When I read the part about Rosa and Raul having an accident, I recall them showing up at the hospital at the last moment, and my sister going directly into delivery. Virgil, however, is her son by birth."

"Then who is your son—Miguel?"

"No, not Miguel, nor Sumo. When Rosa called me in the States, she said my son was alive and well. That wasn't the complete truth. My child was alive, but I didn't give birth to a boy. I had a daughter. And she was adopted by Dr. Zurate's head nurse."

"Marci's your daughter?"

"Uh huh. Why would she deny me, Paulita?"

"I don't know, Leigh. Hey, yes, I do. Marci doesn't know she's your daughter."

"You think so?"

"Of course. Now I understand some of the changes made on those medical records you got from her home. Marci didn't make them—her parents did to keep her in the dark."

"But why?"

"That I don't know, but I know you can't tell Marci."

"Why not?"

"She and Virgil couldn't get married if it became known they were first cousins. She isn't denying you, but you must deny her."

"I must pretend I don't know? How the hell can I do that? And why should I? Don't answer that, Paulita."

"You want to bring unhappiness to your own daughter? If you tell her the truth, that's what it will mean."

"I told you not to answer that. Okay, damn it, I'll let you know what I decide. Keep this under your hat, Paulita. You too, Max."

Chapter XXXXVI

When they returned to guerrilla sub-headquarters, Marci, Dan and Sonia were watching Cory Aquino's inauguration on the rebel-controlled television station. Marci switched channels. Marcos—also claiming victory—was having his own inauguration. The channel suddenly went off the air. As they waited for it to come back on, the phone rang. Paulita answered, listened a few moments, then hung up.

"Miguel says the American Ambassador advised Marcos to leave the Philippines before the country was plunged into a bloody civil war."

"Hope he takes the advice," Dan said.

Leaving Dan, Paulita and Sonia to watch television, Leigh and Marci went to see Virgil. They stayed the rest of the afternoon, talking with him and his doctor. On returning to the office, Leigh was still uncertain what to do. She kept glancing at Marci, debating with herself. Should she pretend to believe the story her daughter had told her? Marci, her daughter. It was difficult to think in those terms. A newscast interrupted her thoughts.

Marcos had left the country. Leigh hugged Dan, then kissed him before embracing the others, lingering a little longer with Marci, looking into her eyes. Sonia opened a bottle of champagne.

As they toasted victory, Leigh asked, "Is your offer of marriage still open, Dan?"

"Always," he replied. "I figured something drastic would have to happen to get you to leave the Philippines, but I hadn't expected Marcos would be overthrown by People Power."

"There's something I must tell you, Dan."

"Are you pregnant?"

"How did you know?"

"I can see it on your face, and in your eyes. You're more beautiful than ever, Leigh."

"Why don't you two get married here?" Paulita asked. "This is the first time I've been witness to a proposal, and I'd like to be at the wedding. So would all your friends, Leigh. I'll make all the arrangements. What do you say?"

Leigh looked at Dan with raised eyebrows. He shrugged. Leigh nodded. Paulita hugged them. Marci held back.

"Don't worry," Leigh whispered to her. "The discussion we had about Virgil will remain our secret. You and my nephew are invited to the wedding."

"Thanks, Leigh." Marci smiled. "We've got to go to the hospital in the morning and be there for Virgil when he comes out of surgery."

"Yes, he'll need moral support."

"News reporters are giving all the credit to diplomats and the courageous people who stood up to the Army," Paulita said. "They deserve most of the accolades, but if soldiers hadn't held their fire, courage and diplomacy would have been useless. Your Virgin Mother balloons were responsible."

"That was a magnificent con job, getting them to believe they had a visit from on high, wasn't it? Dan should get credit for putting them up."

"Not me," Dan replied. "They picked me up before I could get one balloon airborne."

"But who could have done it? Soldiers?"

"They destroyed the balloons when they arrested me."

"How about the dude you met on the plane?" Leigh asked.

"I took all he had."

"Then who?" Paulita asked. "We've had too many reports of the Virgin Mother saying... Oh, my God."

Silence fell over the room. Sonia, Marci and Paulita, gaping in misty-eyed wonder, crossed themselves. Clutching rosary beads to their breasts, they dropped to their knees.

Her flesh tingling warmly, Leigh took Dan's hand, led him to the window. She had returned to the Philippines to find a son she had thought dead. And she had found a daughter, but couldn't acknowledge it without bringing unhappiness to that daughter. Leigh sighed. All right. Marci would never know Leigh was her birth mother. It would be hard, but she could live with that.

Gazing into the starry moonlit heavens, Leigh recalled what Virgil had said. "Have you lost all faith in God, Auntie Leigh?" If she had, it was fully restored at that moment.

"Soldiers saw the Virgin Mother, Dan. Notwithstanding the new life in Virgil's legs and the one inside me, that was the real Miracle of EDSA."

THE END

About the Author

William Newton Edwards has a Bachelor of Science degree in History from the University of Southern Mississippi. For over two decades, he flew jet fighter planes in the U.S. Air Force. He has been stationed at air bases in the United States, England, France, Germany, Turkey, India, China, Japan, Korea, Vietnam and the Phillippines. Among his decorations are two Distinguished Flying Crosses, a Bronze Star, and eight Air Medals. Colonel Edwards started writing while in the Air Force, and has concentrated on fiction since retiring. *The Miracle of EDSA* was written because of his admiration for the extraordinary courage of the Filipino people, in their quest for freedom from the yoke of tyranny. A widower for nine years, the author is now married to Mila Esguerra, former diva with the Manila Opera House, and sings with her choir, the San Francisco Bay Area Cultural Group.